Creepy Competition

Relieved that she had made it to the Chamber of Commerce in time to register for the Haunted House Contest, Amy stopped outside the half-open door to catch her breath. Her chest was heaving and she had a pain in her side.

As her heart stopped beating so fast, she became aware of voices coming from inside the office. A woman was saying something about filling out an entry form, and a girl—

Amy caught her breath. She knew that voice! Suddenly she remembered where she'd heard the word *contest* before. Kristin—who was in the office talking right now—had said it just before Valerie started the scuffle over the bench at lunch today. They'd been trying to distract Amy and her friends so they wouldn't find out about the contest, so they wouldn't be able to enter it and win. But they were *not* going to get away with it!

Shoving open the door, Amy rushed into the office. "You sneaks!" she exclaimed.

Amy's Haunted House

Amy's Haunted House

Susan Meyers

Troll Associates

Published by Troll Associates, Inc. Little Rainbow and Always Friends Club are trademarks of Troll Associates.

Printed in the United States of America.

10 9 8 7 6 5 4 3 2 1

Amy's Haunted House

Chapter 1

Amy Chan was sick and tired of being teased!

It had started at breakfast with her brother Alex. "Ooh, if it isn't Little Miss Muffet," he'd hooted, looking up from his Cheerios as she'd slunk into the kitchen. "Looking for your tuffet?"

Naturally her brother Brendan, who always followed Alex's lead, had chimed right in. "She's not Miss Muffet. She's Little Bo Peep looking for her sheep," he'd chortled, ducking as Amy hurled a bagel at his head.

Even her oldest brother, Mitchell, who was a senior in high school and old enough to drive her to school on bright October mornings like this when both her parents left early for work, hadn't been able to resist. "You should be wearing a name tag today, Amy," he'd said as he dropped her off in front of Redwood Grove Elementary School just minutes before the tardy bell started ringing.

"No one's going to recognize you otherwise."

If only he'd been right! If only every kid in Mr. Crockett's fifth grade class—including her friends Cricket Connors, Meg Kelly, and Brittany Logan—hadn't turned and stared as she'd slipped through the door of Room 5A, clutching her precious backpack (which she was going to need later) and trying to look inconspicuous. If only Michael Brady, sitting at the desk across from hers, hadn't burst out with a startled, "Amy Chan? I don't believe it!" and dorky Melanie Partridge, sitting behind her, hadn't whispered, "Oh, Amy, you look so sweet." If only she'd been able to become invisible. If only her mother hadn't become temporarily insane and forced her to wear a dress—a pink ruffled dress with puffy sleeves and a lace collar—to school!

Amy, as everyone—especially her mother—knew, was a girl who *never* wore dresses. She wore sweatshirts and sweatpants, T-shirts and jeans. She liked red and bright yellow and navy—the colors of the Redwood Grove Junior Soccer League—not icky pink and baby blue. So what if it was school-picture day and half the girls in class were just as dressed up as she was? So what if the pink monstrosity she was wearing had been sent to her by her grandparents all the way from Hong Kong? Amy didn't care about any of that. She just wanted to look like herself. She just didn't want to be teased. Not by her brothers, not by her classmates—not by anyone.

And now this!

She stared unbelievingly at the piece of notebook paper in her hand. It was nearly lunch time and she'd just returned from the auditorium where Mr. Crockett had been sending the class, in groups of six, to have their pictures taken. Now that it was over, now that the photographer had captured her in all her pink glory on film, she was finally beginning to feel better. Soon I'll be out in the school yard, laughing and joking and eating lunch with my friends. Soon I'll be out of this stupid pink dress, she thought as she picked up the paper lying on her desk. When she unfolded it, the words written on it leaped out at her.

> Dearest Amy,
>
> You're a vision of loveliness. I can't get you out of my mind. I dream about you night and day. Love and a zillion kisses.
>
> XXXXXXXXX
> Mark Sanchez

Amy's face suddenly felt like it did when she'd been playing soccer all afternoon on a hot summer day. Her cheeks were blazing. She thought she could feel sweat popping out on her forehead. Had anyone else seen the note? She looked nervously over her shoulder at Melanie Partridge, but Melanie was busy chewing on a strand of her stringy brown hair and scraping bubble gum off the cover of her science book. Amy took a deep breath. Then, trying to act as if nothing out of the ordinary had happened, she glanced across the room at Mark Sanchez, the cutest boy in class. He was picking wax out of his ear. But when he felt Amy's eyes upon him, he stopped, shot her an embarrassed look, and then buried his face in his science book.

Amy quickly lowered her eyes, too. Her heart was pounding. Of course, she wasn't interested in Mark. She wasn't like all the other girls in class who simpered and giggled whenever he turned his big brown eyes in their direction. She wasn't interested in boys, period. Not with three bratty older brothers at home to remind her of what they were really like. But still . . .

She looked at the paper again. The ink was purple, the *i*'s were dotted with circles, the capital letters were embellished with curlicues, and the loops on the *y*'s were as fat as balloons. It didn't look like a boy's handwriting. In fact, it looked like—

Suddenly Amy saw red. She crumpled the paper into a ball and glared across the classroom at her friends—her supposed friends—Cricket Connors and Meg Kelly. The two girls were sitting next to each other in one of the six-desk work groups Mr. Crockett had set up last week. When they saw her looking in their direction, they clapped their hands over their mouths and giggled.

Amy knew they'd seen the look on her face when she'd glanced at Mark. She knew they'd seen for a moment—just for a moment—that she thought the note was really from him. Her face got hot all over again just imagining Cricket and Meg composing those ridiculous sentences, writing them on the piece of notebook paper with Cricket's purple felt-tip pen, and then sneaking the paper onto her desk while she was out of the room.

Was Brittany Logan in on it, too? Amy looked at the beautiful, tawny-haired girl sitting in front of Cricket and Meg. No. She didn't think so. Because as the two girls struggled to stifle their giggles, Brittany turned around, a puzzled expression on her face. Cricket, her eyes sparkling mischievously, leaned forward to whisper something in her ear. Brittany looked confused, then concerned. She glanced at Mark, and then at Amy. Her lips started to mouth a question.

But Amy had had enough. She was not going to sit here, trapped in this stupid pink dress, being made fun of by her friends for one moment longer.

She raised her hand and waved it in Mr. Crockett's direction. When he didn't seem to notice her, she blurted out, "Mr. Crockett, can I go to the girls' room?"

The teacher, who'd been holding up a chart with pictures of marine mammals on it, frowned and glanced at the clock on the wall above the chalkboard. Amy knew he was thinking that it was almost lunch time and that she could certainly wait.

"I really have to go," she said, trying to sound desperate. "Now."

Michael Brady made a rude noise.

"That's enough of that, Michael," Mr. Crockett warned. "All right, Amy, you may go," he said. "But the rest of you, stay put. We've got ten more minutes before lunch. That's plenty of time to learn a few things about scientific classification." He turned back to the chart. "Now who can tell me what kind of marine mammal a sea lion is?"

Amy knew the answer. Pinniped. But this was no time for showing off. As hands shot up all around her, she grabbed the backpack she'd stowed beneath her desk when she'd arrived at school and slipped out of her seat. Then, without another glance at her "friends," she slung the pack over her shoulder and dashed out the door.

The girls' room was just down the hall. Luckily it was empty. Amy checked the stalls just to make sure, then dropped her backpack on the floor and leaned against the wall to catch her breath. Her image, reflected by the mirror above the sinks, was reassuringly familiar, in spite of the pink dress. She liked the way she looked. She always had. Sturdy, with round cheeks, dark eyes, and shiny black hair pulled back in two ponytails. She liked her compact body and the solid way she stood on the ground. Her arms and legs were strong, she could run fast, and it wasn't easy to knock her over. It wasn't easy to get the better of her, either. Not even by writing stupid fake love notes. Cricket and Meg would soon find that out! But first she had to get out of this dress.

Quickly, she undid the pearl-colored buttons that

reached from the collar to the waist. She would have ripped them off except that she knew she was going to have to wear the dress again when her grandparents came to visit. That was one of the things she'd mentioned when she'd argued about the dress with her mother last night. "Why do I have to wear it for school pictures?" she'd protested. "Why can't I just wear it when they come to visit next week?" When none of my friends will see me, she'd thought.

But her mother, usually so reasonable, wouldn't listen. "Lots of girls will be wearing dresses tomorrow, Amy," she'd said. "You won't look a bit out of place. And of course you can wear it when your grandparents come to visit, too. I just want to make sure they have a nice picture of you in it. A picture they can show to their friends in Hong Kong."

Yeah, Amy had thought, a *fake* picture. A picture that doesn't look anything like *me.* But she hadn't dared say it. Not when she saw the look in her mother's eyes. Remembering that look, she felt a twinge of guilt as she unzipped her backpack and pulled out a pair of jeans and her favorite blue sweatshirt. Her mother didn't know that she'd brought them to school. Amy had hit upon the idea after Mrs. Chan had left to teach an early-morning aerobics class at the Workout Workshop. But how could she object? Amy had worn the dress to school. She'd had her picture taken in it. That seemed like enough. She didn't see why she had to go around looking like Little Miss Muffet all day!

She pulled the dress over her head and dropped it on the floor. Then she scrambled into her jeans and sweatshirt. She was already wearing her comfortable old tennis shoes—the school picture wouldn't show her feet after all! Amy looked at herself in the mirror again. Much better! Cricket never would have written that sappy note if she'd been dressed like this. It wouldn't even have occurred to her.

Thinking of the note made Amy angry all over again. It wasn't that she minded being tricked. She could take a joke as well as the next person. And it wasn't just that she'd felt embarrassed. After all, if Mark hadn't written the note, if he didn't even know it existed, there was nothing to feel embarrassed about. What really bothered her was the way Cricket and Meg had been sitting there together, whispering and giggling at her expense. It wasn't fair! They were supposed to be friends, all four of them—Cricket, Meg, Brittany, and Amy—the founding members of the Always Friends Club. Surely that meant they shouldn't be ganging up on each other!

The club, which Amy thought was the most exciting thing that had happened in a long time, had been started by Cricket and Meg. Meg had moved to Redwood Grove from Los Angeles at the beginning of the school year, and she and Cricket had discovered that their mothers, who'd both grown up in Redwood Grove, had been childhood friends. Best of all, they'd had a club—an Always Friends Club—that carried out all kinds of fun, money-making projects. The club members would take turns thinking up projects, work together to carry them out, then pool the money they earned and select one girl (by picking her name out of a hat) to spend it. That way, each club member had a chance of receiving more money than she ever could have earned on her own.

It was a terrific idea. Cricket and Meg had immediately decided to start a club of their own and had asked Amy and Brittany to join. The four girls had already carried out a couple of successful projects. Now it was Amy's turn to think one up. After struggling for weeks, discarding one idea after another, she'd finally come up with what she thought was a good one. Of course she hadn't worked out all the details, and she hadn't told the other girls about it yet, either. She'd been waiting for the meeting that was to be held at her house tomorrow. But now . . .

Maybe I just won't tell them, she thought, making a face in the mirror. A vision of Meg and Cricket laughing at her—Cricket, who used to be *her* best friend—popped into her mind. Maybe I'll make them beg me to let them in on it. Maybe—

Suddenly the lunch bell rang. Amy jumped. She'd forgotten it was nearly lunch time. Quickly she grabbed the pink dress from where she'd dropped it on the floor. Any minute now the restroom would be full of girls making a quick stop before hurrying out to the school yard for lunch. Trying not to think of what her mother would say, she wadded the dress up—ruffles, puffed sleeves, lace collar, and all—and stuffed it into her backpack. She was just zipping the bag shut, listening to the sound of laughter and shouting from the hall outside and thinking about how she could get even with Cricket and Meg, when the door burst open and a familiar voice exclaimed, "Aha! I thought we'd find you in here."

It was Cricket. Her curly red hair, bright orange shirt, and yellow leggings reflected like flames in the mirror. She poked her head back out into the hallway and shouted, "She's here! Come on!" Then she wheeled around to face Amy again. "Neat trick," she declared admiringly, taking in Amy's sweatshirt and jeans. "I knew you couldn't be that desperate to go to the bathroom, but I don't think Mr. Crockett guessed. Now, I know what you're going to say," she rushed on, holding up her hands as Amy took a step in her direction. "That note wasn't fair. But we just couldn't resist. I wish you could have seen your face when you read it! You're not angry, are you?"

"Yes, I am!" said Amy. Somehow, though, with Cricket standing right there in front of her, the words didn't come out quite as forcefully as she'd hoped they would.

The truth was, it was hard to be angry with Cricket Connors. She was always so cheerful and full of high spirits. She and Amy had been friends since the fourth grade, when Amy had moved to Redwood Grove from San Francisco. Cricket had taken her under her wing then, just as she'd taken Meg under her wing now, and made her feel like she'd lived in Redwood Grove all her life. Amy and Cricket had been through a lot together—like having chicken pox at the same time, and getting their bikes stolen from in front of the supermarket, and being tormented all through fourth grade by two of the snobbiest girls in school. Still, that didn't excuse all this stupid stuff about Mark Sanchez. And it didn't excuse Cricket and Meg for conspiring against her!

"I think you and Meg were mean," Amy said now, putting her hands on her hips and sticking out her chin just as Brittany Logan and Meg Kelly burst into the girls' room.

Meg didn't look quite as pleased with herself as Cricket.

Brittany looked downright worried. "Please don't fight!" she cried, stepping between Amy and the other two girls. Brittany was always worried about people fighting. Her main goal seemed to be for the whole world to be friends—something that Amy was sure wasn't possible. "I told them it wasn't funny," Brittany said earnestly now. "No one likes to be teased like that."

"Are you really upset?" asked Meg. Her face, which was usually friendly and open, clouded over.

Amy noticed that she was wearing the same flower-print dress she'd worn on her first day at Redwood Grove Elementary. She remembered how nervous and out of place she'd seemed then, and suddenly it occurred to her that maybe Meg was the one who felt left out. She was new to Redwood Grove, and she'd left all her old friends in Los Angeles—especially a best friend named Jenny. She hadn't known Cricket anywhere near as long as Amy had. Maybe she was even a little bit jealous. Amy could certainly sympathize with *that*! She opened her mouth to say something, but Cricket beat her to it.

"Of course she's not upset," she said, slipping her arm through Amy's. "She knows we were just kidding. She can take a joke. Anyway, it's all Mark's fault for being so cute," she added. "He shouldn't have such long eyelashes and dreamy eyes, not to mention all that curly dark hair. Admit it, Amy," she teased. "You've noticed him, too."

"I have not!" declared Amy. It wasn't quite true. Even a girl who thought boys were a pain couldn't help noticing someone as handsome as Mark Sanchez. But she didn't plan on acting like an idiot over him. She turned quickly away from Cricket—who had a knack for reading minds—and leaned down to pick up her backpack. As she did, she suddenly remembered something. "Oh no. My lunch," she groaned, picturing it sitting on the kitchen counter at home. "I forgot to bring it!"

"No problem," said Cricket, shoving open the girls' room door and herding Amy and the others out into the hall. "I'll share. But only if you promise to forgive Meg and me!"

Chapter 2

Amy didn't like to think of herself as someone who would sell out for a peanut butter sandwich, but Cricket's lunches were definitely a cut above that. Her mother ran a catering business and she always sent Cricket to school with delicious leftovers from wedding buffets, garden club parties, and elegant black tie dinners. On any given day, there were likely to be miniature quiches, marinated mushrooms, pasta salads, or grilled chicken wings, to say nothing of her famous chocolate-dipped coconut macaroons, lemon tarts, and brownies. Amy's stomach rumbled hungrily just thinking about what might be in Cricket's lunch box today.

"All right," she agreed, trying not to look too eager. "But no more fake letters. You've got to promise not to do that again!"

"Don't worry," said Cricket.

"We won't," said Meg.

"I won't let them!" declared Brittany fiercely. "But what I want to know, Amy," she added as they headed out to the school yard, "is why you changed out of that dress. I really liked it."

"You did?" Amy looked at Brittany suspiciously. Was this more teasing? But Brittany herself was wearing a peach-colored dress with a lace collar that was every bit as icky as the pink dress Amy had stuffed into her backpack. "Are you serious?" she asked. "You actually liked it?"

"Yes," replied Brittany. "I saw a dress almost exactly like it in the window of a big department store in Paris this summer. *C'est très* . . . I mean . . ." She blushed as she always did when she lapsed into French. "I mean . . . it's very fashionable."

If Amy had been anyone but Amy, she would have taken that as a compliment. Brittany's mother was a famous fashion designer—Adrienne Logan—and Brittany had lived in Paris and gone to a fancy Swiss boarding school. She could speak French as well as English and she always looked as if she'd just stepped out of the pages of a fashion magazine—even if she was wearing just a T-shirt and jeans. If anyone knew about fashion, it was Brittany Logan. But of course that didn't matter to Amy.

"Well, I thought it made me look like an idiot!" she said, though she couldn't help feeling a twinge of guilt at the way she'd stuffed the dress into her backpack. Maybe she should take the dress out and hang it up somewhere. It still would have been wrinkled, though. It wasn't a sensible piece of clothing like a nice pair of sweats!

"I only wore it because my mother forced me to," she explained as they headed across the noisy school yard, past the foursquare and tetherball courts to the bench beneath the big pine tree where they always ate lunch. "She's gone sort of crazy getting ready for my grandparents' visit. She's been scrubbing floors and cleaning drapes and moving the furniture around. She made Alex and Brendan get their hair cut, and she told Mitchell that if he dares wear his gold earring while they're here he won't be able to drive the car for a year. She even banished Midnight, our poor old cat, from the house because he sheds so much. I have to feed him out in the yard."

"Lucky you don't have a dog like Buster," said Cricket. "I've started taking him to obedience class, but that doesn't do anything for his shedding. Your mother would really go nuts if he was around."

"I don't even want to think about it!" said Amy. Buster was the big, shaggy white dog that Cricket had adopted after the Always Friends Club held a dog wash a few weeks ago. His owner—a sweet little old lady—had broken her hip and couldn't keep him any longer. By giving him a home, Cricket had saved him from being sent to the animal shelter. Buster was full of love and energy and lots of woolly white fur. He was definitely not a dog her mother would appreciate right now!

"Maybe you should save all that fur that falls out," suggested Meg, as they reached the bench. "My grandmother has a friend who makes yarn out of dog hair. She could knit it into a sweater for you," she said, sitting down.

"Or a sweater for the new baby," said Brittany, sitting down beside her. Cricket's mother was going to have a baby in the spring, and all the girls were excited about it. "You could dye it pink or blue, depending on whether it's a boy or a girl."

"Yeah, and get some of those cute little teddy bear buttons," said Amy, as she and Cricket sat down, too. Now this is the way things are supposed to be, she thought. All of us together on our favorite bench. No one staring at me because I look like a pink-frosted cupcake! Even Mark Sanchez was safely out of the way. She'd seen him as they crossed the school yard, hanging out with a group of boys near the basketball hoops. He'd been wearing a yellow yard monitor sash, which meant that he'd be busy for the rest of lunch hour, breaking up fights and seeing that kids threw their garbage in the trash bins. She didn't feel like running into him after all that stupid talk about his eyes and his hair. What if she blushed or, worse yet, giggled? She'd never hear the end of it from Cricket and Meg!

"I don't know about a baby sweater," Cricket said now, opening her lunch box.

Amy stopped thinking about Mark as the smell of teriyaki chicken—her favorite—floated up to her nose.

She thought she caught a glimpse of strawberry tart, too.

"Buster might get confused. Dogs live by their nose. If the baby smelled like a dog—But enough about Buster," Cricket interrupted herself. She started passing out her mother's special jumbo black olives stuffed with cream cheese and walnuts. "What I want to know is when you're going to tell us, Amy."

For a moment, Amy wasn't sure what she was talking about. Then she remembered: the project! She knew they were all dying to find out what she'd thought up. Cricket had been trying to pry it out of her all week, ever since she'd first called the meeting for Saturday. But that didn't mean she had to give in so easily. If they could tease her, she could tease them. "Tell you about what?" she asked innocently.

"Oh, come on, Amy," said Brittany, opening her lunch box and taking out a meatloaf sandwich. "You know what she means. You can't make us wait until tomorrow. It's too cruel!"

Meg didn't say anything, but Amy knew that, of all of them, she cared about the next project the most. Cricket and Brittany were interested, of course, but they'd already gotten their chance to spend the club money. Brittany, whose name had been picked from the hat after their first project, had used hers to buy a camera to take pictures for the club scrapbook. Cricket, whose name had been chosen after their second project, was spending hers on Buster, who was turning out to be a very expensive dog!

That left Amy and Meg. Amy wasn't sure what she'd spend the money on, except maybe sports camp next summer. But Meg had more immediate plans. She wanted to buy an airplane ticket for her friend Jenny so she could fly up from Los Angeles to visit over Christmas vacation. It was already the end of October and Meg was getting worried about whether they'd be able to earn enough in time. Still, Amy couldn't resist drawing out the suspense.

"Well, I don't know," she said slowly, popping an olive into her mouth. "After what you guys did to me . . ."

That was too much. "No fair, Amy!" Meg exclaimed. "Cricket and I apologized. Give us a hint. Just one little—"

She was interrupted by a sudden angry shout.

"Hey, what do you think you're doing here?"

Amy looked up. Two girls—two all-too-familiar girls!—from Mrs. Hamilton's fifth grade class, which usually ate lunch at a later hour, were storming across the school yard toward them.

"Uh-oh," Cricket muttered. "Valerie and Kristin. Double trouble."

"What?" Meg said. She looked questioningly at Cricket and Amy. But before either of them could begin to explain about Valerie Taylor and Kristin Lee—the girls who'd tormented them all through fourth grade—the gruesome twosome was upon them.

Valerie, who was tall and thin and certain that she was better than everyone else, looked down at the girls sitting on the bench as if they were annoying little fleas. "You can't sit here," she declared.

"That's right," said Kristin, tossing her long black hair over her shoulder like a movie star. "This is *our* bench. We always sit here."

Amy couldn't believe it. What nerve! For a moment, she was so astonished that she couldn't respond. Obviously the lunch schedule had been changed because of picture-taking. Valerie and Kristin probably did eat on this bench during their normal lunch hour, but that didn't mean they had a claim on it now. It didn't mean they could just toss Amy and her friends off!

Cricket and Meg seemed dumbstruck, too. Only Brittany managed to speak. "I . . . I don't understand," she said, looking confused. "We sit on this bench every day. I've never seen you here before."

"Oh, really?" said Valerie, raising her eyebrows. "Well, you're seeing us now."

"That's right. Just who do you think you—" Kristin began. Then she stopped. "Hey, wait a second," she said. "I know you. You're the rich girl. The one who comes to school in a limousine."

"No, I don't! I mean . . ." Brittany's face turned red. She *had* come to school in a limousine a couple of times—one that her father's company had leased for him—but she didn't like to be reminded of it. "That is . . . I . . . I don't always," she stammered. "You see—"

But Amy had had enough. "Leave her alone,

Kristin!" she exclaimed, recovering her voice and leaping to her feet. It was one thing for the gruesome twosome to pick on her and Cricket. They were used to it. But picking on Brittany—especially for something that wasn't her fault, like being rich—was too much! She clenched her hands into fists, glad she wasn't wearing the pink dress now. Her mother wouldn't appreciate her getting it torn as well as wrinkled!

But Kristin wasn't about to let it come to that. She took a quick step back. Maybe she was remembering the time Amy had pulled her off the monkey bars by her hair after Kristin had spat a wad of chewed-up crackers down on her head. Or maybe she was remembering how Cricket had locked Kristin and Valerie in the janitor's closet after they'd stolen Amy's lunch and fed it to the seagulls that hung around the school yard. Of course, all that had been when they were younger. None of them did things like that now, but there was no sense taking chances.

"What's the matter?" said Valerie, braver than Kristin. "Can't your little friend speak for herself?"

"Valerie," Amy warned. "You'd better—"

Cricket was on her feet by this time, too. "That's enough," she cautioned. "We don't want to get into trouble for fighting in the school yard." She placed a restraining hand on Amy's arm. As she did, a small metal heart attached to her bracelet snapped loose and fell to the ground.

Valerie swooped down on it like a hawk. "What's

this?" she said, grabbing the heart from where it had rolled beneath the bench and holding it up. "Something from your boyfriend?"

"Give me that!" cried Cricket, making a grab for the heart.

Valerie held it behind her back. Kristin, glad to put a little more distance between herself and Amy, slipped around and took it from her.

"It's an I.D. tag," she said. "Just like my dog's. But what's this Always Friends stuff?" She read the words engraved on the tag along with Cricket's name. "Wait, don't tell me. I know. It's that stupid club we've been hearing about."

That brought Meg and Brittany to their feet, too.

"You mean the one that did the dog wash?" said Valerie.

"That's right," replied Amy, snatching the heart from Kristin. She passed it to Cricket, who quickly put it into her pocket. Amy's own heart was attached to her key chain and tucked away safely in the backpack beneath her desk. Meg and Brittany had heart tags, too. Each was engraved with its owner's name and the name of the club. And they actually were dog I.D. tags. Cricket had ordered them when she'd had one made for Buster. But Valerie and Kristin didn't need to know that.

"I guess you think you're pretty smart," said Valerie scornfully. "Washing all those dogs and making all that money."

"Yeah. You probably think you're going to win the contest, too," Kristin said. She was about to go on, but Valerie stopped her with a furious glance and a sharp jab in the ribs.

"Hey, look!" she exclaimed. "No one's sitting on the bench!"

Amy wasn't sure what happened next. Someone shoved her, but whether it was Valerie or Kristin, or maybe Cricket or Meg trying to get back on the bench, she couldn't tell. All she knew was that suddenly she was on the ground, arms and legs were flailing around her, the bench tipped over, and a yard monitor's whistle blew. Feet pounded toward her, and a hand reached down to grab her. And Amy found herself looking up into Mark Sanchez's big brown eyes.

Chapter

Amy didn't giggle—she would never do that!—but she was sure that she blushed. Or maybe it was just anger at Valerie and Kristin that made her cheeks feel so hot.

"Are you okay?" Mark asked quickly, letting go of her hand as she got to her feet. "What happened?"

Amy felt Kristin's eyes upon her. Fighting got kids into big trouble at Redwood Grove Elementary. Their principal wouldn't stand for it. Notes were sent home, parents were called in for conferences. Amy was suddenly sure, from the nervous look in Kristin's eyes, that *she* was the one who'd pushed her. But if she said that, they'd all have to go to the principal's office to explain. Mark would have to come along as a witness, and Cricket and Meg—who right now were paying too much attention to Valerie and Kristin to really notice who'd come to her rescue—would start teasing her again. Or if they were afraid to do that, they would at least *look* like they wanted to tease her, which would be almost as bad! "Nothing happened," she said quickly. "I just slipped."

"Slipped!" exclaimed Cricket. "You did not, Amy! I distinctly saw Kristin—"

"No, you didn't," interrupted Kristin. "I didn't push anyone. I was just trying to get a seat on the bench."

"That's right," Valerie chimed in. "It's all your fault anyway, Cricket Connors. If you and your friends from your dumb little club weren't sitting on our—"

"Wait a second," said Amy, not about to let her get away with that. "Whose club are you calling dumb? You're just jealous. You wish you had a club as good as ours. You wish you had friends like—" She would have gone on listing all of the things Valerie and Kristin were envious of but she was interrupted by a shout from across the school yard.

"Valerie and Kristin!" Mrs. Hamilton, their teacher, called. "Please come over here. I want to talk to you." Her words were polite, but Amy could see, even from a distance, that she was *not* happy.

"You're in for it now," said Cricket. Everyone knew that Mrs. Hamilton was a stickler for good behavior. She didn't tolerate her students getting involved in school-yard brawls. Neither did Mr. Crockett, for that matter, but luckily he wasn't outside right now.

Valerie looked like she was considering scaling the fence and taking off, but she managed to pull herself together. "Come on," she said haughtily, grabbing Kristin by the arm. "We don't have time to stand around here arguing about a stupid old bench. We've got better things to do!" And with that, the two of them flounced off, looking as if they were going to a tea party with the queen of England rather than to a stern lecture from their teacher.

Meg stared after them, a look of astonishment on her face. "I don't believe it!" she said. "Who *are* those girls? Why do they have it in for you?"

"Who knows? Bad karma, I guess," groaned Cricket, who believed in things like that. Amy liked more concrete explanations, but she had to admit that in this case, the idea that some people just weren't destined to get along—that there was bad karma between them—might be the best explanation. "It's a long story," said Cricket. "I'm not really sure how it all started, but . . ." And forgetting for a moment the dispute over the bench, she launched into a lengthy account of all the torment she and Amy had endured at the hands of the gruesome twosome.

Mark, who'd been fidgeting uncomfortably and looking embarrassed, saw his chance. "Well, if you're sure you don't want to report anything . . ." he said, edging away.

"Don't worry, we don't," replied Amy quickly. She knew she should thank him, even though he'd just been doing his yard monitor job, even though she knew he didn't care the least little bit about her. But before she could get the words out of her mouth, he'd dashed off.

He was halfway to the basketball courts before Cricket noticed him. "Oh, my gosh!" she exclaimed, breaking off in the middle of her story. "That was Mark Sanchez!"

She looked like she was about to say more—probably something about Mark's big brown eyes—but Amy didn't give her a chance. She was *not* going to listen to another word about Mark Sanchez. She didn't want to hear anything more about Valerie and Kristin, either. Those two weren't worth wasting another second on! And she knew exactly how to stop it.

"Eyeballs!" she exclaimed.

"What?" Cricket looked at her as if she'd suddenly gone crazy.

Meg and Brittany, who had put the bench back in place while Cricket was talking and were now gathering up their spilled lunches, stopped what they were doing and stared.

"It's a hint," Amy said, sitting down on the bench as if nothing had happened. She took Cricket's lunch box from Brittany and dug out a piece of chicken. "That's what you wanted, isn't it? A hint about our next project."

It worked like a charm. Within seconds everyone was sitting on the bench again. No one was talking about Valerie and Kristin, and no one was teasing her about Mark. Cricket seemed to have forgotten all about him.

"Eyeballs?" she repeated. "What kind of hint is that? I don't get it."

"Then how about guts?" Amy slurped up a noodle from the Szechuan pasta salad Cricket's mother had packed. "Lots of slippery, slimy guts."

"Yuck!" said Meg.

"And blood," Amy went on. "Can't forget blood. We can squirt it all over—"

"Stop!" Brittany dropped her meatloaf sandwich, dripping with ketchup, back into her lunch box. "What kind of project is this? It sounds disgusting."

"It is," said Amy proudly. "You're on the right track. Disgusting and scary." She glanced at Cricket and Meg. She could see from the look on their faces that they'd suddenly guessed what it was.

"Oh, Amy, what a terrific idea!" exclaimed Cricket. "I can just picture it. We'll have a great big bowl of eyeballs and plenty of guts. We can use vegetable oil to make them slimier and—"

"Stop!" said Brittany again. She looked sort of green. "What are you talking about? What is this project?"

"You mean you haven't guessed? Come on, Brittany, think," said Meg. "It's the end of October, right? Amy's idea is something scary, something disgusting . . ." She looked at her expectantly.

Brittany frowned and looked back just as expectantly.

Suddenly Amy realized what was behind the puzzled

expression on Brittany's face. "Wait a second," she said. "Brittany, have you ever been in a haunted house?"

"A haunted house? Well . . . no," Brittany admitted. "That is, I don't think so. Of course, my mother has a friend who lives in a castle in Scotland that's supposed to be haunted, but I've never been there. But what's that got to do with this? Are we supposed to find a house around here that's haunted?" She looked more confused than ever. "Is that your project?"

Amy shook her head in amazement. She shouldn't have been surprised, but she was. She could see that Cricket and Meg were, too. Brittany Logan was always surprising them, sometimes with the things she *did* know—like where the Maldive Islands were, or what year Marie Antoinette got her head chopped off—and other times with the things that she *didn't* know. Those were mostly ordinary, everyday things that any kid who'd grown up in America took for granted—like what TV shows were most popular, or where to get the best pizza, or . . . how to make a haunted house.

"You'd better explain, Amy," said Meg. "Tell her about using spaghetti for guts and peeling grapes for eyeballs. Of course, we don't have to use grapes," she added. "I knew someone when I lived in Los Angeles whose father was a butcher and he used real cows' eyeballs for his haunted house." She popped one of Cricket's stuffed olives into her mouth as Brittany's eyes opened wide in alarm. "But maybe we shouldn't go that far," she added quickly.

Amy agreed. She wanted their haunted house to be scary and disgusting, not completely repulsive! Otherwise no one would come, and she knew they were going to need a lot of customers to earn the $100 that was the club goal. "Okay, Brittany, let me explain," she said. "The idea is to rig up a house with all kinds of scary stuff for Halloween, which is next Friday. You do know what Halloween is, don't you?"

"Of course I do," said Brittany huffily. "I'm not from another planet!"

"Well, I wasn't sure," said Amy. "I mean, I don't know what they do in France and Switzerland and places like that, but here in Redwood Grove, Halloween is a big deal. There's a party at the Recreation Center and lots of people make haunted houses for trick-or-treaters to go through. Some families have been making them for years. One of the best ones is—" She was about to say Mark Sanchez's, whose family always went all out for Halloween, but she stopped herself just in time.

Luckily Cricket didn't seem to notice. "It's lots of fun, Brittany," she said, taking over the explanations from Amy. "My family did one a few years ago. That was before my mother started her catering business, of course. Now our house is sort of one big kitchen—especially on holidays when my mom has a lot of orders—so we can't do it anymore. But Meg's house would be perfect, wouldn't it, Amy?"

She was right. Meg—along with her mother and

little brother Kevin—was living in her grandparents' big old house in the redwoods until her mother could find them a place of their own. The house was already sort of spooky looking. It had lots of rooms, and a big front porch that would be perfect for jack-o'-lanterns. There was even a secret attic, which was where Meg and Cricket had found the scrapbook that gave them the idea for the Always Friends Club. But Amy didn't want to make a haunted house there. This was *her* project, not Meg's, and she wanted it to be at *her* house.

"Well, maybe," she said diplomatically. "I haven't worked out all the details. But I think my house would be better. It's closer to the center of town."

"True," agreed Cricket. "But would your parents let us do it? I thought your mother was fixing everything up for your grandparents' visit. She wouldn't want them to step into a chamber of horrors, would she?"

"Of course not," said Amy, suddenly imagining the dignified older couple in the photograph that sat on the mantelpiece in the Chans' living room wandering into a house full of spiderwebs and coffins and bowls of cold spaghetti. "But they wouldn't have to," she said. "Halloween is on Friday, and they're not coming until Saturday. By then we'll have everything all cleaned up and put away." She tried to sound confident. It was good practice because that was how she was going to have to sound when she put the idea to her parents. She wasn't at all sure they'd say yes. But she didn't want to think about that now.

"Well, if we can't have it at your house, I'm sure we can have it at mine," said Meg. "If I know my grandfather, he's probably got a Frankenstein costume in the attic that he's dying to wear! There's only one thing though." She hesitated. "I don't mean to sound negative—or greedy—but we *are* supposed to be earning money. You want to go to sports camp, Amy, and I want to bring Jenny up here for a visit. How can we earn enough from this project to do that?"

"I was wondering about that, too," said Brittany. She'd abandoned her meatloaf sandwich and was getting ready to bite into one of the strawberry tarts that Cricket had just passed around. "It certainly sounds like fun, and I'd love to try doing it now that I understand what it's all about. But where does the money come from? Do people usually charge admission for things like this?"

"Well . . . no," Amy admitted uncomfortably. That was one of the details she'd been trying not to think about. "But I'm sure if we make ours good enough, kids will be willing to pay to go through it even if the other houses in town are free. I figured we could charge a quarter, or maybe fifty cents."

Brittany, who was good with numbers, closed her eyes for a second. "Let's see," she said. "There are four quarters in a dollar, so that means . . ." She opened her eyes again. "In order to earn one hundred dollars, we'll need to get four hundred customers!"

"That seems like an awful lot," said Meg.

"I'll say," agreed Cricket, closing her lunch box. "We've never gotten anywhere near that many trick-or-treaters at our house. Even if we charged fifty cents, we'd still need two hundred customers."

"Well, then we'll charge a dollar," said Amy impatiently. She wished she'd figured out all the numbers beforehand, but at least with a dollar, the math was easy. "At that rate we'll just need a hundred kids to go through. That's not so many, is it? Well, is it?" she repeated, annoyed that none of them was nodding in agreement. She knew that a dollar was a lot of money to expect from kids who might not have anything more in their pockets than Tootsie Rolls and candy corn, but still . . . "What's wrong with you anyway?" she demanded. "A minute ago you thought this was a terrific idea and now you're all shooting it down. You're acting just like Valerie and Kristin!"

"No, we're not," Meg objected. "We're just trying to think things through. We can't rush into this. Making a haunted house would be fun, but it might not be a good project for the club. You should have thought of some of these things, Amy, before you—" She stopped herself, but not in time.

Amy felt her stomach tighten. "What are you saying? That I can't come up with a good project?"

"No!" Meg protested. "I mean . . . yes, I'm sure you can, but . . ." Her voice trailed off helplessly.

"All she means is that we should talk about this tomorrow," said Cricket, coming to her rescue. "That's what the club meeting's for, isn't it? Now let's not waste any more of our lunch hour. Who's for tetherball?" She jumped up quickly, followed by Brittany, who grabbed Amy's arm.

"Come on, Amy, you can teach me how to really wrap it around the post," she said, showing more enthusiasm for sports than she'd ever shown before. "We'll figure out all this stuff tomorrow. No point in fighting about it now."

Amy, who'd had enough of arguing for one day, let herself be dragged away. But she couldn't help being mad at Cricket and Meg. After she'd been nice enough to forgive them for writing that stupid note—and for laughing at her, too—the least they could do was refrain from picking her project apart!

Fortunately, tetherball made her forget her anger, at least while she was playing. That was one of the things she liked about sports. You could get outside yourself and not think about a lot of dumb little things. But when lunch hour was over she was glad, for the first time since Mr. Crockett had set up the new work groups, that she was sitting on the opposite side of the classroom from Cricket and Meg. She was even glad when Mr. Crockett asked her to stay after school.

"I wonder what he wants," said Cricket, as she and Meg, followed by a worried-looking Brittany, cut across the classroom after the dismissal bell rang. "I hope it's not about that Valerie and Kristin business. You don't suppose that Mark . . ." She glanced out the doorway to see Mark heading down the hall with a bunch of his friends. "No, I'm sure he wouldn't have told," she went on, not seeming to notice the expression on Amy's face. "It must be about those tests we took, or maybe—"

"Cricket," Meg warned

"Should we wait for you?" asked Brittany, glancing nervously at Amy.

"Don't bother," Amy said coolly, gathering up her backpack and heading for Mr. Crockett's desk. "I'm sure you've got better things to do. And so have I!"

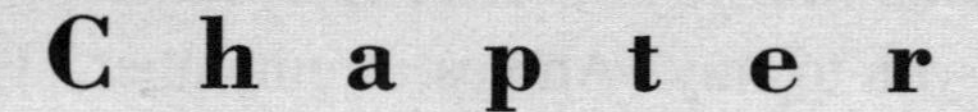

Chapter

"Troubles with your friends?" asked Mr. Crockett, looking up from the papers spread out on his desk.

"No. I mean . . . yes, I guess so," said Amy glumly. It wasn't easy to keep things from their teacher. Sometimes she thought he had eyes in the back of his head! Not that he would have needed them this time. He could hardly have missed the way Brittany and Meg, a look of dismay on their faces, had started after her. Nor the way they'd stopped, discouraged, when she didn't even glance their way. And he'd certainly heard Cricket call out a hopeful "See you tomorrow, then?" as the girls left the room. And he couldn't fail to have noticed that Amy hadn't said a single word in reply.

"Well, these things have a way of working themselves out," he commented philosophically. "Now let me see . . ." He ran his hand over his white beard, which made him look sort of like Santa Claus. "Why did I ask you to stay? Ah yes, I remember." He reached into his desk, pulled out a white business-sized envelope, and handed it to her. "I'd like you to take this home to your parents," he said.

Amy felt her stomach sink. She should have known this was coming. All of her problems with spelling had surfaced this year, along with her confusion about stuff like where to put the apostrophe in possessives and what was the difference between "its" and "it's." Then there was the seven times table that she'd never quite mastered. . . .

She stared at her parents' names on the envelope. Wasn't this how her brother Brendan had found out he was flunking algebra—by a letter sent home to their parents—and how her brother Alex had found out that if he didn't shape up fast he was likely to be left back in the fourth grade? Amy had been in kindergarten then, but she remembered the uproar when her parents got that letter. Alex had to get a tutor and drop out of Little League until he improved his grades.

A vision of herself tearfully turning in her soccer shirt popped into her mind. But this couldn't be anything like that, she thought quickly. It was too early in the year. It had to be those tests that Cricket had mentioned. They'd taken them a few weeks ago, and there'd been plenty of parts that she'd struggled over—words she'd never heard of and number sequences she couldn't quite figure out. Of course, there'd also been those little diagrams that you had to sort of flip around in your mind, matching ones that were flat with ones that were three-dimensional. Those had been fun, but—

"Amy, are you listening?"

"What?" She was vaguely aware that Mr. Crockett had been talking, but she'd been too caught up in her own thoughts for his words to sink in. "Uh, yes . . . I mean, no," she admitted. No sense making things worse than they already were by lying. "What were you saying?"

"I was asking whether you like to build things."

"Build things?" Amy frowned. What did that have to do with failing a test? "Do you mean like the dolphin?" she asked. The class had just started making a dolphin out of papier-mâché to go with the black-and-white killer whale that last year's fifth grade class had made. The whale was hanging from the ceiling above their heads right now and the dolphin was destined to join it.

"I was thinking more of buildings," Mr. Crockett said, smiling slightly. "I was wondering if you liked to play with blocks when you were in kindergarten. Or if maybe you designed the layout of your room at home, or made yourself a doll house."

"Well, I'm not really interested in dolls," replied Amy honestly, still wondering what he was getting at. "I liked blocks, though. I used to build terrific castles and skyscrapers. And I did make myself a model zoo last year. I plotted it all out beforehand on graph paper. My brother Mitchell uses that paper in his drafting class. That class seems so interesting," she added. "I'm going to take it when I get to high school." *If* I get to high school, she thought, suddenly remembering what might be in the envelope.

"Mmm . . . very interesting," said Mr. Crockett, nodding his head. "There must be something to these things." He regarded her thoughtfully, the way he sometimes did the iguanas that lived in a terrarium at the back of the classroom. Then he smiled, as if to declare the interview ended. "Well, now, I won't keep you any longer," he said. "Don't look so worried. Just put that envelope in your pack and be sure to give it to your parents."

But what is it? Amy wanted to ask. She would have if she thought she'd get an answer, but she knew that she wouldn't. Maybe she should just take his advice and stop worrying. At least he hadn't said anything like, "You don't really want to go to high school, do you?" or "Forget about going on to sixth grade."

It could be an invitation to Parent Night, she thought hopefully. Or maybe a letter asking her father, who was a doctor, to visit the school on Career Day. It might even be a note telling her parents what a great student she was, or how much Mr. Crockett liked having her in class. She didn't really believe that, of course, but thinking it made her feel better. As she tried to stop worrying, she unzipped her backpack and a puff of pink fabric popped out like a cloud of cotton candy.

Mr. Crockett looked surprised. Then he laughed. "Ah, the dress!" he said, as she stuffed it back in along with the envelope. "I wondered what had happened to it. You looked very nice in it, Amy, but I don't blame you for changing. I can't imagine walking around in something like that all day. Though I did dress up as Mother Goose one Halloween. I thought my beard added a nice touch."

Amy smiled in spite of herself at the idea of Mr. Crockett in a long dress, with a bonnet on his head and a beard on his chin. She could just imagine him walking around town, frightening little children by reciting, "Hey diddle diddle, the cat and the fiddle."

"Yes, Halloween is my favorite holiday," he said. "I was a pretty good Frankenstein's monster one year, too. Though no one seemed to find that as scary as my Mother Goose. By the way, are you entering the contest?"

"Contest?" Where had she heard that word before? "What contest?"

"You mean you don't know about it?" Mr. Crockett seemed surprised. "Well, I guess the Chamber of Commerce hasn't done a very good job of publicizing it then. They did put out a flyer, though. Wait a second. I have it here somewhere." He rummaged through the papers on his desk. "Ah, here it is!" He dug out a sheet of bright orange paper and handed it to Amy.

As Amy read the words, she drew in her breath in surprise. She didn't think she could speak.

"It's a good idea, isn't it?" said Mr. Crockett, not seeming to notice the change that had come over her. "I don't know why they never did it before. I'd enter, but it wouldn't be much fun with my kids all off in college. You really should consider entering though, Amy. I'm sure that with your special abilities you could—"

But Amy didn't let him finish. "Mr. Crockett, could I keep this?" she blurted out, recovering her voice. She didn't know what he meant by special abilities and she didn't care. All she knew was that she had to get to the Chamber of Commerce office. And fast!

"Sure, take it," he replied generously. "And if you do enter, maybe you could ask your friends to help you. Working on a project like this would be a good way to patch things up, don't you think?"

Amy had no time to reply. She was already halfway out the door. She barely remembered to call out a quick "Thanks, Mr. Crockett!" before she dashed down the hall, past the auditorium where the photographer was packing up his equipment, past the school office, and out the front door.

Would her friends still be there? No. Only a few kids were lingering around the front steps of the school, waiting for rides home. The bus that Brittany took was gone, and there was no sign of Cricket or Meg. Not that she'd really thought there would be. She could hardly have expected them to wait for her after the way she'd behaved. But now everything was different!

She held up the flyer, suddenly afraid she might

have imagined what it said. But she hadn't. It was right there in bold black print, next to the picture of a spooky-looking house with bats and ghosts flying from its windows: FIRST ANNUAL REDWOOD GROVE HAUNTED HOUSE CONTEST!

Amy could hardly believe it. It was enough to make her think that all that crazy stuff Cricket was always talking about—karma and kismet and destiny—was true. Because if Mr. Crockett hadn't kept her after class, if he hadn't given her the envelope to take home, if her pink dress hadn't popped out of her backpack and reminded him of Mother Goose and Halloween, if she hadn't worn the pink dress to school . . . But it was too much to think about!

Hands trembling slightly, she checked the words at the bottom of the flyer again. *Entries must be made by 4 PM, Friday, October 24.* That was today. Twenty minutes from now! And then, the most important words of all, *First Prize: $200.* She closed her eyes, though she knew she was wasting valuable minutes, then opened them again. The words were still there. "First prize: two hundred dollars!" she read out loud.

Amy *had* to get there in time. She flew down the steps. Her feet scarcely seemed to touch the sidewalk as she raced toward the center of town.

Luckily, Amy knew exactly where the Chamber of Commerce office was: right next to the post office, just a few blocks from the Workout Workshop where her mother was teaching an afternoon class. She never would have been able to make it in time if she'd walked, and she probably wouldn't have made it if she'd been less of a runner. But Amy always won races on Track and Field Day at school and she was one of the fastest players on her soccer team, so it wasn't surprising that she reached the Chamber of Commerce office in fifteen minutes flat, just as the clock on the post office next door read five minutes to four.

Relieved that she'd made it in time, she stopped outside the half-open door to catch her breath. Her chest was heaving and she had a pain in her side. Her cheeks felt almost as hot as they had when she'd read that phony love note from Mark Sanchez! Would he be entering the contest, too? she wondered. She hadn't had time to think about that, but Mark's haunted houses were famous, and lots of other kids made good ones, too. There was bound to be plenty of competition.

It was a sobering thought. So sobering that for a moment she wasn't aware of the voices coming from inside the office. Then, as her chest stopped heaving and her heart stopped beating so fast, her ears tuned in. A woman was saying something about filling out an entry form, and a girl—

Amy caught her breath. She knew that voice! Suddenly she remembered where she'd heard the word *contest* before. Kristin—who was in the office talking right now—had said it just before Valerie started the scuffle over the bench and Amy wound up on the ground. So *that's* what they'd been up to! They'd been trying to distract Amy and her friends so they wouldn't find out about the contest, so they wouldn't be able to enter it and win. But they were *not* going to get away with it!

Shoving open the door, Amy rushed into the office. "You sneaks!" she exclaimed.

Valerie and Kristin, who were standing at the counter filling out an entry form, spun around at the sound of her voice. "You!" Valerie said, her eyes opening wide. "I thought you didn't know—I mean, how did you find out—" She whisked the entry form off the counter and hid it behind her back. But it was too late.

"Ah, another contestant," the plump, pleasant-looking woman behind the counter said, seeing the flyer in Amy's hand. "You're just in time." She took out another entry form and a pen and placed them on the counter.

"No, she's not!" exclaimed Kristin. She pointed to the clock on the wall. The long hand had just moved past the twelve, making the time 4:01.

"Oh, that." The clerk dismissed the clock with a wave of her hand. "It's always at least five minutes fast, sometimes ten. We don't pay any attention to it. Besides," she went on, sizing up the situation between Amy and the other two girls, "if she was too late to enter, you would be, too. I don't believe I have your completed form in my hands yet, either."

Kristin's cheeks turned red. She grabbed the entry form from Valerie and thrust it at the clerk. "There," she said. "You have it now!"

"Yes," said Valerie, recovering her poise. "So go ahead and enter, Amy. It's a free country. But I wouldn't count on winning." She shot a sly glance at Kristin.

"That's right," Kristin agreed quickly, returning the glance. A mysterious look came over her face. "We've got secret ammunition!"

And before Amy could ask what they were talking about, the two of them disappeared out the door.

Chapter

Secret ammunition? Amy didn't like the sound of that, but then, she didn't like the sound of anything Kristin and Valerie said! She turned to the clerk at the counter. "Did they really finish filling out the form?" she asked, hoping that maybe they'd made a mistake or left something out—something that would disqualify them.

The woman put on her glasses, which were dangling from a chain around her neck, and studied the form that Kristin had handed her. "Looks like everything's here," she said after a moment. "If you want to enter, you'd better get busy filling one out, too. That clock isn't all that fast." She winked conspiratorially. "In fact, it's not fast at all, but I couldn't let those two get away with keeping you out of the contest. I remember when I was your age I had to deal with a couple of girls like that—Myrna Marks and Stephanie Pitt. Oh, they were awful. You wouldn't believe some of the things they did!"

Amy thought she probably would, having dealt with Valerie and Kristin, but she didn't have time to trade war stories. As the clerk chatted on, recalling her childhood trials and tribulations, she picked up the pen and began filling in blanks on the entry form. The first was labeled "Name of entrant" and she didn't hesitate to write "Always Friends Club," followed by her own name in parentheses. She was sure that even though Cricket and Meg and Brittany had picked apart her idea of doing a haunted house as a project, they'd be eager to make one once they found out about the contest. The address was another matter. Should she write in her own, even though she hadn't gotten permission? Of course, she *could* run over to the Workout Workshop right now and ask. But somehow she didn't think that barging in right in the middle of her mother's class was the best way to put her in a mood to say yes!

The clerk noticed her hesitation. "Now be sure you write in the correct address," she said, interrupting her account of school days with Myrna and Stephanie (who really did sound every bit as awful as Valerie and Kristin). "We're printing up a map this weekend for the judges to use. Once that's done, we can't allow any changes."

That settled it. She couldn't very well write in Meg's address without Meg asking her grandparents first. What if they said no? Besides, she didn't want *her* haunted house to be at Meg's place—even if Meg did have a secret attic and a spooky setting and a porch that was made for jack-o'-lanterns. Amy was sure that her own house would be just as scary once they got it decorated. Quickly, trying not to think of what would happen if her parents said no, she wrote in her address and handed the form to the clerk.

The woman looked it over. "Ah, I see you're entering as a club," she said, smiling approvingly. "That should be fun. I had a club when I was a girl. Let's see now, who was in it? Marsha Crumley, Allison Weber, and Judy Finch. I still take exercise classes with Judy at the Workout Workshop." She looked at Amy's name on the entry form. "Say, you're not related to Helen Chan, are you—that dynamo of a woman who teaches there?"

"She's my mother," replied Amy proudly. She wasn't exactly sure what a dynamo was, but it sounded like dynamite and that certainly described her mother's style when she was trying to get a class moving. "She's been teaching aerobics at the Workout Workshop ever since we moved to Redwood Grove. I'm supposed to meet her there after her last class this afternoon," she added, glancing at the clock, which now read 4:25. She had a feeling that the clerk was one of those people who would go on chatting forever if you didn't stop her, or at least plan your escape. Picking up her backpack and the contest flyer, she began edging toward the door.

"Well, she's one terrific teacher," the woman went

on admiringly, not seeming to notice that she was losing her audience. "Of course I can never can keep up with her. She must have springs in her legs instead of muscles! Judy's better at it than I am, and even she . . ."

But Amy was already out the door. She called out a quick "Thanks a lot," and then, feeling like she was floating on air, headed down the street toward the exercise studio. She scarcely noticed the shops that she passed—the pet shop with its window full of cute little kittens that normally she would have stopped to play with, the florist's shop bursting with orange and gold chrysanthemums, fall leaves, and miniature pumpkins, the toy shop, the book store, the dry cleaners, and Elmer's Ice Cream Emporium with its red-and-white-striped awning shading the window and the mouth-watering smell of hot fudge wafting out the door into the afternoon air.

I did it! she thought. All the exciting ideas she'd had when she first thought up the haunted house project—before her friends had started criticizing it—came rushing back to her. There were so many terrific things they could do. They could make tombstones for the front yard out of cardboard shirt boxes and hang pillowcase ghosts from the trees. They could make the house dark and spooky inside by screwing blue lightbulbs into all the lamps and hanging black curtains over the windows. Cricket probably had lots of that kind of stuff left over from the haunted house her family had made a few years ago.

I'll call her as soon as I get home, she thought. Then she realized that she didn't want to tell Cricket or any of the other girls about the contest over the phone. She wanted to tell them in person at the meeting tomorrow so she could see the looks on their faces when they found out what she'd done!

She was thinking so hard about what that would be like that she almost missed turning down the block where the Workout Workshop was located. She caught herself just in time, turned the corner, and then, checking for traffic, dashed across the street to the exercise studio. She stopped for a moment outside the big white door with WORKOUT WORKSHOP stenciled across it, to look at the bright orange flyer again. Everything was there, just the same as before—the house with the bats and ghosts flying out the windows, the deadline for entries, and the magical words *First Prize: $200.*

She still couldn't believe it. That was twice the club goal. If they won, she and Meg could both have their names picked out of the hat. She could start packing her tennies for sports camp and Meg could run straight to the travel agency to buy her friend Jenny a plane ticket for Christmas. Brittany, whose turn was next, wouldn't even have to think of a project if she didn't want to!

Of course in order to win, they'd have to beat all the other kids who'd entered—including Valerie and Kristin, with their secret ammunition, and maybe Mark Sanchez, too. There might even be some grown-ups who'd signed up—maybe even some from the Redwood Grove Drama Society who had experience with sets and lighting and putting on shows. That was an unsettling thought. Was it fair to have grown-ups competing against kids? Shouldn't there be separate categories for each?

Frowning, Amy leaned against the workshop door and checked the flyer again. But before she could even begin to look for any mention of categories, the door suddenly gave way. Someone was opening it from the inside.

"Hey, wait!" Amy cried, struggling to regain her balance. But it was no use. Her feet had already slipped out from under her. She fell backward, the flyer flew out of her hand, and she landed with a thud on the floor.

For a moment, she was too stunned to do anything. Then she blinked, shook her head, and for the second time that day looked up into a pair of big brown eyes. Mark Sanchez!

"Amy!" he exclaimed. "Gosh, I'm sorry. I didn't know you were out there." He reached down to help her up.

A sound dangerously close to a giggle—or at least an awkward little laugh—escaped Amy's lips. "That's okay," she said, scrambling to her feet without taking the hand Mark held out to her. "My mother teaches here." It was a stupid thing to say, but it was all she could think of. "Aerobics. Upstairs," she added, even more pointlessly, since the ceiling above their heads was shaking with the sound of music and the pounding of feet. The only things on the ground floor level where they were standing were the changing rooms and showers.

"Oh . . . well . . ." Mark looked a bit awkward himself. "I guess my mother's in her class, then," he said. "I was supposed to meet her here but they're not done yet. I thought I'd just go out and get—" All at once, he stopped. Because his eyes, which he'd kept directed at the floor rather than at Amy, had suddenly fallen on the bright orange flyer that had fluttered from her hand. He snatched it up. "The contest!" he exclaimed, staring at the flyer almost hungrily. "Are you entering? I couldn't believe it when I heard about it," he rushed on, not waiting for an answer. "How could they hold one this year of all years? Just my luck!"

"What do you mean?" said Amy. She wished her pulse would stop racing so fast. What was the matter with her? Mark was just a boy. No different from her brothers. But she didn't recall ever getting such a funny feeling in her stomach around Alex or Brendan or Mitchell! "Aren't you going to enter?" she asked.

"Can't," replied Mark. He looked discouraged. Amy noticed for the first time that the hair at the back of his neck curled over his collar in shiny dark ringlets. "Our house is being remodeled. It's a total wreck. We've got all kinds of great stuff—coffins and skeletons and severed heads and things—stored in the garage, but there's no way we can set up a haunted house this year. I just hope they do the contest again next year."

"Well, it does say 'first annual,'" Amy pointed out, struggling to pull herself together. She should be turning cartwheels at the news that Mark wasn't going to be in the contest. It would make their chances of winning a hundred times better. But somehow standing here alone with him, with the music throbbing above their heads, made her brain feel sort of fuzzy. "Annual means they plan to do it every year, doesn't it?" she said, hoping she sounded more normal than she felt.

"Yeah, I guess it does," agreed Mark, brightening a bit. "And we're bound to be done remodeling by next year. Though my mom and dad say they're afraid it's going to go on forever!" He looked at Amy and smiled shyly. "Those idiots from Mrs. Hamilton's class were really giving you a tough time today, weren't they," he said.

Amy was glad to have the subject changed. It was easier to be angry at Valerie and Kristin than it was to feel all mushy and weird inside. "They're such jerks!" she said vehemently. "Anyway, thanks for breaking it up."

"Well, I had to because of being yard monitor," Mark said honestly. "But I know you could have handled it yourself. You're strong. I've watched you play soccer."

"You have?" Amy hadn't thought Mark Sanchez

had ever noticed her at all, much less that he'd seen her at her best, which was on the soccer field. That's why that stupid note Cricket and Meg sent her had been such a shock—until she realized it was a fake. But she wasn't going to think about *that* now. "So you go to soccer games," she said, trying to sound casual. "You've seen me . . . I mean my team?"

"Sure. Lots of times," replied Mark. He seemed to be trying to sound casual, too. "You're really good." He grinned and Amy noticed that he had a dimple in his cheek. "Well . . . I guess I'd better get going," he said, handing her the flyer. Amy watched the dimple disappear. "I thought I'd head over to Elmer's and get an ice cream or something. Do you . . ." He hesitated as if he wanted to say more, but then seemed to think better of it and turned quickly away. "See you around," he called as he ducked out the door. Then breaking into a run, he disappeared down the block.

Amy stared after him. She had a crazy feeling that he'd been about to ask her to go to Elmer's with him. But that was ridiculous! Why would Mark Sanchez ask her to go to Elmer's for ice cream? And what if he had? Would she have gone? And if she had gone, what if someone—Cricket or Meg, for instance—had been there? What if they'd seen her—seen *them*—there together?

She didn't want to think about it. If she'd been teased before when she'd barely realized Mark existed, what would it be like now when—But enough of that.

Grabbing her backpack, Amy stuffed the flyer into one of the side pockets. Overhead, the music picked up and the feet started pounding faster as the class shifted into high gear. Amy knew the routine. She'd helped her mother choreograph it. She could see all the moves in her head. And suddenly she wanted nothing more than to be up there with the class, jumping and strutting and stretching her muscles. Anything to put Mark Sanchez out of her mind!

Chapter

Springing into action, Amy dashed into the changing room and headed straight for the locker where she kept her leotard and tights. Mrs. Chan let her join her classes whenever she wanted, as long as she kept up with the routines and didn't get in the regular students' way. That had never been a problem, since Amy knew the steps and could move quicker than any of them. But today she wasn't so sure. Would she be able to make it through the complicated routines they were doing? Her mind was so confused, even the smell of sweat and dirty gym socks didn't seem to clear it!

She opened the locker and stared into it, thinking of what had just happened. Mark *had* been going to ask her to go to Elmer's. She was sure of it. He'd watched her play soccer. He thought she was strong. He didn't like all those stupid girls who were always giggling over him. He liked—But she couldn't let herself think it. She couldn't let her brain get all gooey over Mark. She had too many other things to think about, too many other things to do!

Quickly, shoving Mark and his dimples and curly dark hair to the back of her mind, she pulled off her sweatshirt and jeans. She grabbed her tights and leotard and wriggled into them. Then she stuffed everything—sweatshirt and jeans, her backpack with the pink dress, the haunted house flyer, and the letter from Mr. Crockett inside—into the locker and slammed the door shut. The noise of metal hitting metal seemed to help. Her brain clicked into gear the way it did when the referee blew the whistle at the start of a soccer game, and she ran up the stairs to the studio and slipped into place at the back of the class.

Her mother, wearing a rainbow-striped leotard, was in the front facing the floor-to-ceiling mirrors that stretched across the wall. She was moving hard and fast, her short, straight black hair bouncing as she shouted encouragement to the sweat-drenched women twisting and jumping in the rows behind her. Between steps she caught a glimpse of Amy in the mirror and smiled.

Amy smiled back. And as always, when she saw her mother working, she felt a sudden surge of pride. She was so strong, so confident, so full of energy. Nothing ever seemed to get her down or wear her out. Right now, though the class was at the height of the aerobic phase of the workout and Mrs. Chan was glistening with sweat, she hardly seemed tired at all.

That's how I want to be when I grow up, Amy thought as she quickly found her place in the routine and began moving to the beat of the music. Soon she was stretching and jumping and turning in unison with her mother and the other women in the class. It was a great feeling, everyone working together like that, and she was sorry when the music slowed and the class moved into the cool-down phase. She liked the relaxation period, though, when they got to lie on the floor and stretch their arms and legs slowly as her mother talked in a soothing voice about taking deep breaths and being at one with the world. When it was over, and the class had given itself a round of applause, Amy's body felt light and her head was clear. She could barely remember all the confusing thoughts that had been swirling around in it just a short time before.

Mrs. Chan grabbed a towel and wiped herself off. "You were really looking good there, Amy," she said, giving her a hug as they followed the rest of the class down the stairs and into the changing room. "Did you notice how I added some steps in the middle of the routine? Do you think it works better?"

"Yes, I do," said Amy. She liked it when her mother asked her opinion—especially since Amy knew she really valued it. "I think it improves it a lot. But I had to concentrate hard to keep up. That lady from the Chamber of Commerce would never have—" She stopped herself just in time. This wasn't the time or the place to start explaining about the contest.

Luckily, her mother, who'd turned to answer a question from one of her students, didn't seem to notice.

While the two women talked, Amy opened her locker and started to pull off her leotard. She was going to have to bring up the haunted house soon. She needed to get permission before the meeting tomorrow. But she wanted to wait for just the right moment. Maybe after she'd helped with the dishes or taken out the garbage!

She reached into the locker, pushing aside her backpack to get out her sweatshirt and jeans. Suddenly she remembered the dress. Maybe she should put it on now, so that her mother wouldn't know she hadn't been wearing it all day. That might make it easier when she asked about building the haunted house. Of course, the dress would probably be kind of wrinkled. Her mother was sure to notice that. Maybe it would be better to just come clean and admit that she hadn't wanted to walk around school looking like a strawberry sundae. That she hadn't wanted to be teased anymore, not by Alex or Brendan, or by anyone in class like Michael Brady or—

All at once, Amy found herself thinking of Mark Sanchez. Had he noticed the dress? He hadn't said anything, but of course he must have. What could he have thought, seeing someone he admired for playing soccer going around dressed like that?

The thought of Mark Sanchez decided things for her. She was not going to put on the dress again, not when she might run into him on the street—or even right here at the Workout Workshop if he came back to pick up his mom. She'd forgotten that one of those panting, sweating women in the class was Mark's mother. She suddenly imagined Mark bursting into the locker room and decided not to change into her sweat-shirt and jeans either. She'd leave on her leotard and tights and try to convince her mother to do the same so they could clear out of here—fast!

Mrs. Chan was still talking as Amy grabbed her backpack from the locker and tried to force Mark Sanchez out of her mind. "Don't worry," she was saying encouragingly to her student. "You'll catch on to those new steps in no time."

The woman sighed. "Well, I hope so," she said. "I'm fed up with all this remodeling on our house, and I need the exercise because I've been doing a lot of nervous eating. It's going to take real willpower to resist an ice cream cone when I go over to Elmer's to pick up my son. Of course, they've got frozen yogurt, too. That's a lot better for you than ice cream."

"Yes, it is," agreed Mrs. Chan. "I love that peach melba flavor they make. In fact, I wouldn't mind having some right now. How about it, Amy? Should we go over there with Mrs. Sanchez?"

Amy stared. This woman was Mark's mother! She had to think fast. She was *not* going to go to Elmer's

and meet Mark—not in the company of their mothers!
"Uh . . . well . . . I don't know," she stalled. "I . . . I'm not very hungry. I don't really feel like having ice cream." Her mother's eyebrows shot up in surprise. "And besides, I . . . I've got a lot of homework," she said quickly. "Why don't we just go home?"

It wasn't a very convincing explanation, especially since Mr. Crockett never assigned homework over the weekend, and even if he had Amy would hardly have done it on Friday afternoon. Her claim of not being hungry was undercut, too, when her stomach suddenly growled loudly. Mrs. Chan looked worried then, and she stayed worried throughout the whole trip home in the car.

"Are you sure you're all right, Amy?" she said as she unloaded the last of the shopping bags and bundles from the back of the car and carried them into the Chans' big chrome-and-black kitchen. She dropped the packages on the table, and for what seemed like the hundredth time since they'd left the exercise studio, reached out to feel Amy's forehead.

"Mom!" Amy protested, squirming away. "I told you I'm fine. I just didn't feel like having ice cream, that's all!"

"But that's so unlike you," said Mrs. Chan, stooping to pick up a shopping bag labeled "Barbara's Bed and Bath Shop," which had fallen to the floor. A stack of pink-and-blue-flowered towels—hardly her usual taste—tumbled out. "I hope you're not coming down with something," she said, piling the towels on the table. "I hear that chicken pox is going around again. That's all we need with your grandparents coming!"

Amy didn't bother to point out that she'd already had chicken pox. Alex was the one who'd missed them, but with four children her mother had a hard time keeping track of who had what. Amy didn't care about that, though. What she wanted to know, now that she'd escaped going to Elmer's and running into Mark, and even managed to avoid being asked about the pink dress, was why she had bought all this stuff!

There was tons of it. Besides the towels—which they certainly didn't need since they already had plenty of them in black and gray and bright lemon-yellow, her mother's favorite color combinations—there was a pale blue throw rug, a patchwork comforter, down pillows, new sheets, placemats, a lamp, and even a shower curtain with butterflies and bluebirds fluttering across it. The whole back of the car had been loaded with boxes and bags. "You must have spent half the day shopping, Mom," said Amy, adding the bundles she'd carried in from the car, along with her backpack, to the stacks already on the table. "Why?"

"Because I'll be too busy to shop tomorrow," replied Mrs. Chan, not quite answering Amy's question as she opened the freezer and took out a package of chicken. She put it in the microwave to defrost. "Brenda's on vacation, so I have to take over all her Saturday classes. Since I'm going to be teaching all day, I was afraid that if I didn't shop now I wouldn't get another chance to buy the things I need for your grandparents' visit. I won't have much time next week, either," she rushed on, starting to tear up greens for a salad, "because I've got to wallpaper the guest bathroom, and then I want to plant ground cover along the front walk. And look—" She dropped the lettuce, picked up a decorating magazine lying open on the counter by the microwave, and flipped to an article on dried flower arrangements. "I thought I could do something like this for the dining room."

She held out the magazine, but Amy hardly looked at it. "Mom," she said, staring in amazement at her mother, who, as far as Amy knew, had never made a dried flower arrangement or wallpapered a bathroom. "You've got to stop acting so crazy! I'm sure Grandma and Grandpa Chan don't care about any of this stuff!"

But even as she said it, she realized she wasn't quite sure. She actually didn't know her grandparents on her father's side of the family very well. They lived in Hong Kong, which was a long way from Redwood Grove—halfway around the world, in fact. Her other set of grandparents—her mother's mom and dad—lived in San Francisco, just across the bay, and she saw them all the time. But she hadn't seen her Hong Kong grandparents since way back when she was in nursery school. She didn't remember much about the visit they'd made then, but she did recall the delicious dumplings her grandmother had cooked and how her grandfather had taken her to the park to build sand castles. And she still had the big stuffed panda bear they'd brought her sitting on her bed. But that didn't tell her whether they cared about towels and shower curtains and ground cover, or why preparing for their visit seemed to have driven her mother out of her mind.

"I am *not* acting crazy," Mrs. Chan protested now. "I don't know why you and your brothers keep saying that. I just want the house to look right. I want everything to go well. But that doesn't mean I'm—" She was interrupted by a sudden loud and forlorn "Meow!" coming from the patio outside the kitchen.

"Midnight!" Amy said, turning to see the Chans' big black cat sitting on the other side of the sliding glass doors. He looked at her pitifully and patted the glass with his paw.

Suddenly something inside Amy snapped. "Mom, just look at him. He's freezing out there!" she exclaimed. "How could you banish him like that? And how could you make Brendan and Alex cut their hair? And force me to wear that stupid pink dress to school. It's not fair!" she said angrily as Midnight meowed again. "Just because Grandma and Grandpa are coming, you want all of us to change our lives. You probably won't even let me make a haunted house on Halloween!"

It wasn't exactly the way she'd planned to ask permission, but the words were out of her mouth before she could stop them. Not surprisingly, her mother's answer wasn't the one she'd hoped for either. "A haunted house?" she repeated, looking at Amy in astonishment. "Do you mean here? On Halloween, the day before your grandparents arrive? Of course not!" Mrs. Chan said. "Whatever gave you such an idea? As for Midnight, he's not freezing. It's sixty degrees outside. And as for the dress—by the way, where is the dress?" she asked suspiciously, looking at Amy as if noticing for the first time that she was still in her leotard and tights. "You did wear it for the school picture, didn't you?"

Amy was still reeling from her rejection of the haunted house. But she couldn't let her mother think that she'd cheated. "Of course I did!" she said. "I wore it for the picture just like I promised, but then I changed into my sweatshirt and jeans. I wasn't going to walk around like Little Miss Muffet all day! It's in here." She unzipped her backpack angrily. "It might be a little wrinkled, but—" She pulled the dress out. It was a *lot* wrinkled, more than she'd expected, and there was some kind of stain on it, too—maybe from the old chocolate bar that had melted in one of the corners of her backpack.

"Oh, Amy!" Mrs. Chan looked at the dress in dismay. "Well, I guess I'll just have to wash it. Or maybe I can take it to the dry cleaners. They'll do a better job. Let's see . . . I could drop it off there on my way to pick up the ground cover." The buzzer on the microwave went off and she rushed to rotate the defrosting chicken. “And I could stop by that new housewares shop at the same time. I saw a lovely teapot there that I think your grandmother would like. Our old one is so—” She stopped, as if she’d suddenly heard what she was saying. She looked at Amy, who was staring at her in alarm, and at Midnight, who was meowing outside the glass door. She stared at the piles of towels and the shopping bags bulging with placemats and pillows and sheets. “Oh, Amy,” she said. “Look at me. I’m not thinking about anything but this visit. You’re right. I *am* acting crazy!” She sank down on one of the chrome-and-black kitchen chairs, leaned her elbows on the table, and covered her face with her hands.

"Mom?" Amy said anxiously. Could she be crying? She thought she heard a faint sniffling sound. But her mother never cried. Amy wouldn't know what to do if she did. "Are you all right, Mom?" she asked, dropping the wrinkled dress on a chair and rushing over to put her arms around her mother. "I could make you a cup of tea."

Mrs. Chan took her hands away from her face. Her eyes did look damp, but she managed to smile. "That would be nice, Amy. Thank you," she said.

Amy rushed to fill the shiny black tea kettle with water. What had happened? Why had she suddenly exploded at her mother like that? She'd made her cry, she'd probably ruined everything.

Quickly, trying not to think of what her mother had said about the haunted house, she put the kettle on the stove and got out a tea bag—orange spice, her mother's favorite—and a mug with *We Love You Mom* printed on the side, a Mother's Day gift from her and her brothers.

It seemed to help. At least Mrs. Chan smiled when she saw it. And her spirits seemed to rise even more when, a few moments later, she sipped the fragrant tea that Amy had brewed and bit into one of the shortbread cookies she'd found in the cupboard. "Ah, that's better," she said as Amy sat down at the table across from her. "I'm so sorry. I know I've got to get hold of myself. I'm fine at the exercise studio when all I have to think about is the music and the moves."

Amy nodded. She could certainly understand that.

"But when it's over," Mrs. Chan went on, "I start thinking about all the things I ought to do to prepare for your grandparents' visit. I guess I just want so much for them to like me. To approve of me."

"Approve of you?" Amy looked at her mother in surprise. Approval was the sort of thing she or her friends might worry about. But grown-ups—especially ones like her mother who managed a house full of teenage boys and whipped classes full of overweight women into shape—weren't supposed to think about things like that. "But of course they approve of you," she said. "Why wouldn't they?"

"Well, I don't think I'm exactly the daughter-in-law they expected," Mrs. Chan said, smiling wryly. She took another sip of tea. "I don't know what they thought would happen when your father came to school in the United States," she said, talking to herself as much as to Amy. "They certainly didn't know he'd meet me. I guess they hoped he'd return home after he graduated. I think they may even have had someone else picked out for him."

"Someone else?" Amy was stunned. "You mean someone else to marry?" It was an incredible thought.

"Of course, I don't really know about that," said Mrs. Chan quickly, as if she suddenly realized that Amy was listening. "Your grandparents are wonderful people, and they've always been very kind to me. When we visited them last year—when your father was speaking at that medical convention in Hong Kong—they were terrific. But their house is so different from ours. Your grandmother has such beautiful things, lovely dishes and tablecloths. She raises orchids and she's a wonderful cook." Amy's mother leaped up to rescue the chicken from the microwave before it stopped defrosting and started cooking. "I've never been great in the kitchen you know, and I always forget to water the houseplants. I don't wear makeup and I'm more comfortable in jeans than in dresses, and . . ."

She went on talking as if glad to get it all off her chest, but Amy was only half-listening. Dad not married to Mom. Her brain seemed to spin inside her head. Mom not married to Dad. But what did that mean? That she'd have a different mother or a different father? Or did it mean that she just wouldn't exist?

She suddenly felt as she had once at camp when

she'd been lying outside in her sleeping bag, looking up at the stars spread out across the night sky. The space they were in seemed so vast, and all at once she'd realized that, lying in her sleeping bag there on the planet Earth, she was in that space, too, and that compared to all that was out there, she was no bigger than a pebble—no, a tiny speck of dust! The same weird feeling she'd had then came over her now. There were millions and millions of people on Earth. How incredible it was that her mom and dad had ever met! And yet if they hadn't met, if they hadn't fallen in love with each other, where would she be? Nowhere. Without them there would be no Alex or Brendan or Mitchell. Without them there would be no Amy!

She shuddered at the thought, then jumped as Midnight let out another loud meow. "Mom, can't we let him in?" she begged, suddenly wondering where Midnight would be if she didn't exist. Would he live next door with the Goldmans? Or maybe down the block with the Lows? Would there be anyone to feed him Tuna-4-Cats dinners or to buy him catnip mice at the pet shop?

"Oh, why not," said Mrs. Chan. "I can't bear to see him so miserable myself." She opened the door and Midnight streaked in, as if afraid that one moment's hesitation might cause the door to be shut in his face again.

Amy scooped the cat up and rubbed her cheek against his fur. His body felt warm and solid and real.

Her mother seemed very real, too, as she gave Amy a squeeze. "Thanks for listening," she said. "I'm much better now, and I promise I'll try to calm down. For starters, I won't wallpaper the bathroom and I'll forget about making that dried flower arrangement." She tossed the decorating magazine into the recycling box. "And maybe I was a little quick to say no. Tell me," she said seriously, crossing to the counter by the stove and starting to arrange the chicken in a baking dish. "What's all this about a haunted house? I seem to have heard someone else—I can't remember who—talking about the very same thing recently. Is there something special going on?"

Amy's heart gave a leap. She stopped thinking about not existing. Her mother was giving her a second chance! Quickly, she dropped Midnight, who dashed into the pantry to look for his cat food. She dug the bright orange flyer out of the pocket of her backpack. She wasn't going to mess things up this time. No losing her temper, no complaining about things being unfair. "It's a contest," she said, holding out the flyer to her mother. "It's being run by the Chamber of Commerce. Cricket and Meg and Brittany and I want to enter it as a club project. They're offering a prize. See." She pointed to the line—the magical line—on the flyer.

Mrs. Chan wiped her hands on a towel and took the flyer from Amy. "Two hundred dollars," she said, looking impressed. "That's an awful lot. Twice what you've earned on your other projects, isn't it?"

"That's right," said Amy, feeling excited all over again. "If we can do it, Meg will be able to bring her friend Jenny up for Christmas and I'll be able to put one hundred dollars toward sports camp. I know you and Dad said I could go, but I don't want you to have to pay for all of it. I want to contribute," she said virtuously. "Just like Mitchell helped pay for his car and Alex and Brendan help pay for their tennis lessons." She wondered if this was a good time to volunteer to do the dishes for a month or to clean out the garage. But she didn't want her mother to think she was resorting to bribery—at least not so early in the game.

Mrs. Chan smiled appreciatively. "Well, that's very good of you," she said. "But this is a contest. You can't count on getting the money. Do you really think you could win?"

"I don't know," replied Amy honestly. "But we can certainly try. I've got it all figured out. We can set things up in the hall and the family room and maybe in one of the bathrooms. We won't have to use the rest of the house at all. We can hang black drapes and cobwebs, have a skeleton leaping out of a closet, and maybe a dead body in the bathtub. And we'll clean everything up," she added quickly, realizing from the look on her mother's face that it might be better not to go into all the details. "When Grandma and Grandpa get here on Saturday, there won't be a trace of it left. I promise. Please, Mom," she said, trying not to sound like she was begging. "You've got to say yes."

"Well . . . I don't know . . ." Amy could see that her mother was wavering. "It does sound like fun," she admitted. "I think your father might be willing to loan you the skeleton from his office. His patients certainly wouldn't miss it." She paused. "Of course, I had been planning on doing a final cleaning Friday night. Alex and Brendan will be safely out of the way at the Recreation Center party and I can never manage to clean with them around. But I suppose . . ." She glanced at the flyer again.

Amy held her breath. Please say yes, she thought.

But instead her mother looked at the flyer more closely. "Wait a second, Amy," she said. "Look at this." She pointed to the line about the deadline for entries. "October twenty-fourth, four P.M. That was this afternoon, before you came to the Workout Workshop. You've already missed the deadline. I'm afraid you won't be able to enter no matter what I say, so—" She stopped and suddenly looked hard at Amy.

Amy knew she was reading her mind. She was almost as good at it as Cricket. Amy tried not to think about how she'd gone to the Chamber of Commerce office and filled in the entry form. She tried not to think of Valerie and Kristin and the plump lady behind the counter who was in her mother's class. But it was no use.

"Amy!" Mrs. Chan said. "You've already entered, haven't you? You didn't wait to get permission. You took things into your own hands and did it!"

"But Mom," Amy objected, forgetting her resolution about not complaining or losing her temper. "I *had* to. I just found out about the contest today when Mr. Crockett kept me after—I mean, when Mr. Crockett gave me the flyer," she corrected herself quickly. No point in going into *that* story now! "There wasn't any time to ask permission. I had to run all the way to the Chamber of Commerce office and when I got there it was five minutes to four and Valerie and Kristin were there!"

"You mean Valerie Taylor and Kristin Lee? Are they going to be in this contest, too?" Mrs. Chan frowned and shoved the dish of chicken in the oven. She knew all about Valerie and Kristin. She and Cricket's mother had spent plenty of time on the phone with each other last year talking about ways to help their daughters deal with the gruesome twosome. They'd even had a run-in with Valerie's mother during Parent Night. Cricket and Amy hadn't been there, of course, but they'd heard that their fathers had to practically drag the women apart.

"Kristin said they were going to win because they had some kind of secret ammunition," said Amy, seeing her chance. "I couldn't let her get away with that, could I?"

"Well, you *could* have," replied Mrs. Chan. "But I have to admit that I probably wouldn't have. In fact, I'm sure I would have done exactly what you did." She shook her head. "You know, Amy, I think that's why we have so many fights. You and I are just too much alike!"

"But what does that mean, Mom?" said Amy, not about to stop pressing her case until she heard her mother say yes. "Does it mean we can do it?"

Mrs. Chan laughed. "You don't give up, do you? Well, I probably really am crazy this time," she said, "but yes! Remember though," she went on, as Amy let out a whoop and threw her arms around her. "You have to promise to clean up everything before your grandparents get here. And of course," she added, "we'll have to check with your father . . ."

But that was no problem. When Dr. Chan arrived home, his briefcase full of medical journals that he planned to read over the weekend, he quickly agreed. "As long as it doesn't interfere with your schoolwork," he said as they sat down to dinner.

Alex, Brendan, and Mitchell—who'd burst noisily into the kitchen just as their mother was taking the chicken from the oven—groaned. "Dad, you say exactly the same thing whenever any of us wants to do anything!" said Mitchell. As the oldest, he had plenty of experience.

"Maybe that's because it's a good thing to say," replied their father calmly. "School comes first. Isn't that right, Amy?"

"What? Oh, yes," said Amy. She reached for a piece of chicken, being careful not to look her mother in the eye. She didn't want her to read her mind this time, because if she did she'd find out about the envelope lying in the bottom of her backpack—the envelope that could mean tutoring every afternoon, no more soccer, and the end of her membership in the Always Friends Club.

There's no reason for them to know about it now, Amy thought, glancing quickly at her parents. She'd almost forgotten it herself. It was easy to forget a little thing like that. In fact, she had a feeling it might be a while before she remembered it again—at least until next Saturday when the contest was over!

Chapter

Telling Cricket, Meg, and Brittany what had happened was even better than Amy had imagined it would be. The girls arrived together the next morning, in Cricket's mother's catering van, and Amy could tell from the moment she opened the door how nervous they were about the meeting.

"My mom sent these cinnamon buns," Cricket said, holding out a plate of sticky-sweet rolls as if they were a peace offering. "She drove us over here on the way to a brunch she's catering. They're still hot."

"Great!" said Amy cheerfully, taking the plate. "Come on in. I've been working on designs for the haunted house!" She saw Meg and Cricket exchange a worried glance. They must have been talking about her in the back of the van, surrounded by cinnamon buns and bagels. They'd probably been trying to figure out how to convince her that her idea for a project was crazy.

"Now Amy . . ." Brittany began anxiously.

Amy pretended not to hear. Carrying the plate of cinnamon buns, she herded the girls into her bedroom. It was a colorful room with a red, yellow, and blue patchwork quilt on the bed, a red beanbag chair in one corner, and posters of gymnasts, soccer players, and other athletes on the walls. Everything was set up for the meeting. Amy had stayed up late making diagrams of the area her parents had agreed they could use. She'd measured the rooms carefully with a tape measure and drawn them to scale on sheets of graph paper she'd borrowed from Mitchell. Then she'd cut out pieces of construction paper in different shapes and sizes to stand for the things they would set up in the house, like coffins, bowls of eyeballs, and buckets of guts. She'd stuck the pieces to the diagrams with wax stick, a kind of waxy glue that didn't dry, so they'd be able to experiment, moving the pieces around until they figured out which arrangement was best. When everything was done, she'd propped the diagrams up on her old painting easel and hung a sign beneath them reading ALWAYS FRIENDS CLUB HAUNTED HOUSE in big red letters.

Cricket and Meg looked at the sign and stole a glance at Amy. Brittany, who'd brought her camera, pushed the flash button and got ready to take a picture, then seemed to think better of it. Maybe this wasn't a scene they'd want recorded in the club scrapbook! Setting the camera aside, she stepped up to the easel and examined the diagrams along with Cricket and Meg. "Amy, you must have really worked hard on these," she said, looking impressed. "But I thought . . . that is, didn't we decide that a haunted house wasn't quite . . ." She looked helplessly at the other two girls as if hoping they'd bail her out.

But Amy didn't give them a chance. She was enjoying her little game, but she didn't want to be too cruel. They'd suffered enough. Besides, she couldn't wait a moment longer to tell them what she'd done! "Don't worry, you don't have to humor me, Brittany," she said, setting the cinnamon buns down on her dresser where Midnight, who was curled up next to the panda bear on her bed, wouldn't be able to get them. "I know all of you thought my haunted house project wouldn't work when I told you about it. But that was yesterday when you didn't know about this!" She pulled the haunted house flyer out from beneath the diagrams where she'd hidden it, and presented it to the girls with a flourish.

Now *that* was the moment Brittany should have captured on film! Amy thought later. Though she would have needed a video camera to record the way the girls' expressions changed from puzzlement to astonishment to excitement in the space of a few seconds, plus a tape recorder to capture their exclamations as they took in the words.

"Don't worry about the deadline," Amy said quickly, seeing Cricket's eyes stray to that line on the flyer.

"We're all signed up. I made it to the Chamber of Commerce office just in time, and I got my parents' permission, too. All we have to do is promise to have everything cleaned up before my grandparents arrive. Luckily, Alex and Brendan are going to a party Halloween night so they won't be around to bug us. Well? What do you think?" she asked proudly.

Meg was the first to answer, and she started by apologizing. "Oh, Amy, I'm so sorry," she said. "This is wonderful!" Her eyes shone with excitement. "I never should have given you such a hard time yesterday. If I'd known there was a contest . . ."

"I'm sorry, too," said Cricket. "Even though we were right about not being able to earn enough money by charging admission to a haunted house," she added honestly. "But how could we have missed hearing about this contest? I'm sure I never saw any of these flyers around town."

"Neither did I," said Amy. "It was just luck that Mr. Crockett gave me this one." She tried not to think of what else he'd given her. The envelope with her parents' names on it was still lying at the bottom of her chocolate-stained backpack. "I guess the Chamber of Commerce didn't do a very good job of publicizing it," she went on quickly, echoing what Mr. Crockett had said. "But that didn't stop Valerie and Kristin."

"You mean *they* know about it?" said Cricket, a look of dismay coming over her face.

Amy nodded. "Afraid so," she said. "They were in

the Chamber of Commerce office when I got there. They tried to keep me from entering by saying I'd missed the deadline. Then, when that didn't work, they said they were sure they were going to win because they had some kind of secret ammunition. I think they must have been bluffing, though. What could they have that would help win a contest like this?"

"Maybe they're going to bribe the judges," suggested Meg, looking worried. "From what I saw yesterday, I wouldn't put it past them."

"I wouldn't, either!" said Brittany. She sat down on the bed. Midnight, who loved attention—especially after being banished to the patio for nearly a week—jumped into her lap. "They could do it by offering to split the prize money with them. I read a mystery book that had a plot like that," she said, stroking the cat's silky fur.

"Well . . . I suppose they *could*," said Amy. "But that would be illegal or something, wouldn't it? A real crime. I don't think even Valerie and Kristin would go that far. Do you, Cricket?"

Cricket didn't answer. She was frowning as if she were thinking hard, or trying to remember something.

"Cricket?" Amy said again. "Did you hear me? Do you think that Valerie and Kristin would—"

Before Amy could finish her sentence, Cricket's eyes opened wide and she exclaimed, "Oh no! Amy, I know what their secret ammunition is. It's Valerie's uncle!"

"What?" Amy wasn't sure that she'd heard right.

"Her uncle," Cricket repeated. "He's the set designer for the Redwood Grove Drama Society! My mother was talking about him just the other day. She catered the opening night party for their new play. It's called *Dracula,* and it's all about vampires. She said the set was terrific—really spooky with lots of great lighting and special effects. And Valerie's uncle designed it all. I'll bet he's helping them make their haunted house!"

Amy couldn't imagine worse news. Of course, she'd thought about the drama society herself yesterday, when she'd been worried about competition, but she'd never dreamed that Valerie and Kristin would have the set designer on their side. "Are you sure?" she said desperately. "I mean about him being her uncle."

"Yes, I'm sure," said Cricket grimly. "And I can just imagine the kinds of things they'll make with his help. Dancing skeletons, ghosts that fly across the room on wires like Peter Pan, all kinds of lighting and costumes and sound effects. They might even use stuff from the *Dracula* set."

Amy's heart sank. It would almost be better if Valerie and Kristin did try to bribe the judges, she thought. At least then, if the Chamber of Commerce found out about it, they'd be disqualified. But there was nothing in the rules that said your uncle couldn't help you.

"Well, I don't think we should be discouraged!" declared Meg. "We don't know for sure that he's helping them. And even if he is, the judges might not go for such a professional-looking job. Lots of times people prefer things that kids do themselves. Like the dolphin we're working on in Mr. Crockett's class. It's going to have some lumps and bumps, but that's part of its charm."

"I agree," said Brittany, before Amy could object that a haunted house wasn't exactly supposed to be charming. "Entering the contest is a great opportunity and it'll be lots of fun, too. We can't quit before we even begin. I'm sure the four of us can come up with all kinds of terrific stuff. And just think of the pictures we'll have for the scrapbook," she added, fingering her camera as if she couldn't wait to start shooting. "Now come on. Stop looking so discouraged and tell me—besides peeled grapes and cold spaghetti, what goes into one of these houses?"

Amy had already put together a list of stuff they could make, like construction paper bats, giant string spider webs, and cardboard tombstones for the front yard. But now, imagining what Valerie's uncle must be cooking up, it didn't seem too impressive. Of course, she thought, grasping at straws, Meg *could* be right. Maybe the judges wouldn't be looking for the sort of stuff you'd find in an amusement-park fun house. Maybe they'd appreciate a more homespun approach.

Meg, not about to give up, took the list from her hand. "Amy, these are good ideas!" she said as she read it. "And I know we can think of lots more. Let's brainstorm like we do in our work groups at school. I'll start. Let's see . . . here's something one of my neighbors in Los Angeles did." She launched into an account of how her neighbor had dressed up as a fortune teller and read trick-or-treaters' palms. "Then to get our treats, we had to follow her into a pitch-black room and reach into a hollow, glow-in-the-dark skull. It was really scary," she said, "especially if you were little. They have skulls just like that at the toy store here in town. I saw them the other day. We could buy one and put peeled grapes underneath the treats so if kids reach down far enough they'll get a real scare!"

"Yes, that would be good," said Amy, her spirits rising as she imagined a bunch of little kids, their knees quaking with fear, reaching into a glowing skull and feeling something slimy beneath the Tootsie Rolls and gumdrops.

Cricket, encouraged by Meg's enthusiasm, began making suggestions for wrapping dolls in toilet paper to make mummies and constructing headless figures out of clothes stuffed with newspapers. After listening for a while, even Brittany got the hang of things and came up with a suitably gruesome idea. "How about this," she said, helping herself to a cinnamon bun. "My mother could get one of those department store mannequins—you know, those figures they display clothes on. Then we could take it apart and strew the arms and legs all over the house. If we painted the ends red they'd look bloody. And maybe we could stick the head on a pike near the front door. They did that with real heads in medieval days," she added with a shiver. "I learned about it in my history class last year."

That started off a whole chain of ideas for taking Barbie dolls apart and scattering their remains among the tombstones, and for making grisly-looking heads out of papier-mâché to decorate the front steps. "I'm not sure about that one, though," said Cricket. "Papier-mâché takes forever to dry, and we don't have much time. We've got to get all this stuff ready by Friday afternoon at the latest and we're starting from scratch. It's not as if we have a whole garage or attic full of stuff that we can just roll out and set up."

She was right, Amy thought, getting worried again. It was going to be hard to build all this stuff in one week. And there was another problem, too. Money. Lots of the things they'd been brainstorming about, like the glow-in-the-dark skull, fake cobwebs and spiders—even the grapes and the spaghetti—would cost money, and right now they didn't have any. They'd donated all the extra earnings from their dog washing project to the county animal shelter. That was a good thing, but maybe they should have kept some for the club treasury. Of course, they might be able to get a loan from their parents. They could repay it when they won the contest. But suppose they didn't win?

Amy did *not* want to think about that. "Maybe we've done enough brainstorming for a while," she said, scrambling out of the beanbag chair where she'd been sitting taking notes. Her hand felt like it was going to fall off from writing so much anyway. "Let's go check out the rooms my parents said we could use. Then we'll have a better idea of what stuff we should make."

Midnight leaped off the bed and followed them as they trooped down the hall to the family room carrying what remained of the cinnamon buns. Mitchell, who'd been holed up in there all morning studying for his college entrance exams, was just gathering up his books when the girls came through the door. Amy quickly introduced Meg and Brittany, who hadn't met him before.

Mitchell smiled. "Well, the room's all yours," he said, cramming his books into his backpack and slinging it over his shoulder. "I'm going to the library to work on the personal essays I have to write for my college applications. You kids don't know how lucky you are," he added, giving Meg a playful wink and stealing a cinnamon bun from the plate she was holding. "Enjoy your youth!"

"Yeah, like you're so old," Amy teased, glad for a moment to be thinking about something besides all the stuff they had to do for the haunted house. "And don't forget what Mom said about that earring," she shouted, as Mitchell, his gold earring safely in place in his ear lobe until his grandparents arrived, disappeared down the hall.

Meg stared after him, a peculiar look on her face.

"That's your brother, Amy?" she said breathlessly, as the front door slammed shut. "But you never said anything about . . . I mean, you never said he was so . . ." She blushed. "So cute!"

"Mitchell, cute?" Amy looked at Meg as if she were crazy. Maybe all that brainstorming had short-circuited her brain. "You've got to be kidding!"

"Oh, but she's right," said Brittany seriously. "He looks a little like one of those actors on that television show about a high school in Beverly Hills. My parents don't like me to watch it," she added, "but sometimes I do."

"You know, that's true," said Cricket. "I never thought of it before, but Mitchell's got that lock of hair that falls down over his forehead. He's always flipping it back just like—"

"Cricket, stop!" Amy exclaimed. "The next thing you'll be telling me is that Brendan is cute."

"Well, I wouldn't go that far," said Cricket, who'd had her share of run-ins with Amy's youngest brother. "But speaking of cute . . ." she said, frowning as if she'd suddenly thought of something important. "I wonder if Mark Sanchez is entering this contest. He made one of the best haunted houses in town last year. We won't stand *any* chance of winning if he enters it, too!"

"Oh, but he's not going to," said Amy. "He told me so himself. He's got a whole garage full of stuff left over from last year, but he can't enter because—" She stopped, but it was too late.

Cricket looked at her in astonishment. "Amy," she said. "When were you talking to Mark?" She glanced quickly at Meg, who was still pink-cheeked from her encounter with Mitchell. "Don't tell me that note we sent you is coming true."

"Don't be ridiculous!" Amy exclaimed. She hoped that her own face wasn't giving her away. "I just happened to bump into him, that's all." No need to explain that she'd actually fallen on the floor at his feet! "His mother takes classes from my mother at the Workout Workshop. He saw the flyer and mentioned that he can't enter the contest because his family's remodeling their house, so . . . so there," she finished lamely.

Cricket looked as if she might have said more, but Brittany didn't let her. "Well, that's good. The less competition, the better," she said, as if declaring the subject closed. "Now, I think I should take some pictures of this room before we decorate it. Then we can have before-and-after photos for the scrapbook."

"Good idea. I'll go get the camera," said Amy, eager to get away from Cricket's prying eyes—to say nothing of her mind-reading abilities. She dashed out of the family room before anyone could stop her and hurried down the hall to her bedroom. Brittany's camera was lying on the dresser where she'd left it after taking a bunch of pictures of Midnight. Amy picked it up, then paused to stare at herself in the mirror.

She was glad to see that she looked the same as always. But what she'd said to Cricket was right. All this stuff about Mark Sanchez *was* ridiculous! Maybe she did sort of like him in the way Cricket imagined, but she didn't want to act like Meg had about Mitchell! In fact, now that she knew more about Mark—how he liked soccer and admired strong people, how he was disappointed at not being able to enter the haunted house contest—she thought he was someone she might like as a friend. But how could you be friends with anyone—boy or girl—if people were always teasing you?

She remembered how she and Cricket had become friends when Cricket had helped her fit in at Redwood Grove Elementary, and how they'd both helped Meg and Brittany to do the same. That's what friendship was all about—helping each other when you needed it. All this giggly stuff spoiled everything!

Behind her, reflected in the mirror, she could see the panda bear her grandparents had given her sitting on her bed, the easel holding her carefully drawn diagrams—and suddenly, a freckled face surrounded by curly red hair.

"Cricket!" she said angrily, turning around. "You'd better not say anything more about—"

"Wait, Amy!" Cricket stopped her. She stepped through the doorway and into the room, an excited look on her face. "I know what you're going to say and you're right. I shouldn't have teased you, especially when—" She paused. "Listen. I have an idea," she said quickly. "Don't say no before you hear it, but . . . well, you know how Mark told you he can't enter the contest and how he has all that stuff stored in his garage? Well, I thought that maybe we could . . ." She hesitated, as if not sure how to go on. "I mean, I don't know if he'd want to work with us. But we could share the prize money. He could have half."

Amy stared at her, the meaning of her words sinking in. Her stomach did a quick flip-flop as she thought of Mark's curly dark hair and brown eyes. She might not be able to act normally when he was around, but it would solve their problems. They wouldn't have to buy things or build all new stuff. They'd give Valerie and Kristin—and Valerie's set designer uncle—a run for their money. And it would certainly be a way of becoming friends.

"I promise I won't do any more teasing," said Cricket. "And neither will Meg. Brittany says we should do it. What do you think?"

What could Amy think? It was a brilliant idea—becoming partners with Mark Sanchez! "Yes! Why not? We'll do it!" she said.

Chapter

Me?" said Mark on Monday morning. "You want me to make a haunted house with you?" He glanced over his shoulder as if afraid that one of his friends might see him standing on the front steps of the school surrounded by a bunch of girls. "Well, gee . . . I don't know," he said, as a group of first graders made their way past them. "I . . . I'll have to think about it."

"No, you won't," said Amy boldly, pleased at the way she sounded—perfectly normal, not the least bit giggly. "Don't waste time thinking. Just say yes."

"Come on, Mark," Cricket urged. "We'll be partners. We can share the prize money."

"Fifty-fifty," added Meg.

"And it'll be fun!" said Brittany. "I'll take pictures of everything and have double prints made so you can have a set for your scrapbook. If you have one, that is. Maybe we could even make you an honorary member of our club."

That was a bit too much for Mark. "Uh . . . no, you don't have to do that," he said quickly, taking a step back. "But maybe you're right about the haunted house." He looked thoughtfully at Amy, who'd put the proposal to him. She'd explained all about the club and about Valerie and Kristin, and told him how they were already signed up for the contest. "I really did want to enter," he said. "And all that great stuff's just sitting there in our garage. How many rooms did you say we could use in your house?"

"Three," replied Amy. "The front hall, the family room, and one of the bathrooms. I guess we could use my room, too. You said you had a fake severed head, didn't you? Maybe we could put that in my beanbag chair. And I found a Halloween book at the library yesterday that suggested putting a skeleton under the bedcovers with a breakfast tray full of moldy food propped up in front of it! My father's a doctor and he said we can borrow the skeleton from his office. And we've probably got some moldy food at the back of our refrigerator. My mom's always putting leftovers in covered dishes and then forgetting about them."

Mark looked impressed, just as he had when he'd told Amy about watching her play soccer. "A skeleton eating breakfast in bed," he said. "Neat! I wouldn't have thought of that. I've got a nice big coffin that my brother helped me make, and a battery-operated hand that waves its fingers, and a whole flock of ghosts that we can run across the yard on wires and pulleys. Last year my grandmother gave me a big black kettle that looks like a witch's cauldron. Maybe we could get some dry ice to put in it and—" He stopped, as if suddenly realizing what he was saying.

"So you'll do it?" Amy prompted.

Mark grinned. The dimple that Amy had noticed the other day at the Workout Workshop appeared in his cheek. "Sounds like it, doesn't it?" he said. "All right then. It's a deal. We're partners!"

Cricket let out a whoop. Brittany looked like she was about to throw her arms around him. But luckily for Mark, who didn't look like he wanted to be hugged on the school steps in broad daylight, the tardy bell started ringing. "We can talk about it at lunch," he said. "Okay?" And with a parting smile at Amy, he dashed off to join his friends, who were hurrying up the steps into school.

Amy's heart was racing. She was glad there was no more time for talk because she didn't know if she could go on speaking so calmly. Cricket, Meg, and Brittany were excited, too. "We did it!" Cricket exclaimed as they dashed up the steps, past the school office, and down the hallway toward their classroom.

"I can't believe it!" said Meg.

"You were really good, Amy," added Brittany. "You explained everything so well."

"Yes," agreed Cricket. "And you know what?" She grabbed Amy's arm and stopped her just outside the door to Room 5A. "Mark is nice. With all that giggling and teasing and talking about how cute he is, I hadn't really noticed. Now I think we're going to be friends—real friends."

Amy thought so, too. She slipped into her seat and glanced across the classroom at Mark. He smiled. Behind her she heard silly Melanie Partridge giggle. But this time she didn't care. She smiled back at Mark. And for the first time since Cricket and Meg had sent her that stupid fake love note she didn't feel embarrassed at all!

Friday seemed to take forever to come. Not that they didn't have plenty to do. They were busy every day making things like tombstones and headless figures and pillowcase ghosts. Meg found some dark velvet drapes in her grandparents' attic that were perfect for lining the walls of the front hall to make it seem like a long, dark tunnel. Cricket found a tape of spooky sound effects, Amy and Brittany worked on witch costumes for them to wear, and everyone—including Alex, Brendan, and Mitchell—peeled grapes.

Mark and his older brother Steve brought all their haunted house stuff over to Amy's house in the back of Steve's pickup truck and stored it in the family room, ready to be set up on Friday before the judging began. "My goodness," said Mrs. Chan when she saw it. "I didn't realize how much there would be." She smiled bravely, but Amy knew she was still worried, not only about the haunted house, but about the arrival of Amy's grandparents.

"I do hope I've managed to think of everything," she said when she picked up Amy and the other girls after school on Friday. Cricket, Meg, and Brittany were going straight to the Chans' house to start setting things up. "Their plane gets in at seven o'clock on Saturday," she continued. "I'm sure they'll be tired so I haven't planned anything for that evening, but on Sunday we can go to San Francisco for dim sum and to ride the cable cars. Or maybe they'd rather have a quiet day at home. What do you think, Amy, should we all go to the airport to meet them or just—"

"Mom," Amy interrupted. "Stop worrying! Everything's going to be fine. The boys and I have it all figured out. We'll all go to the airport to meet them. We'll leave early so we get there in plenty of time. And they're going to love the welcome banner Meg made," she said. Meg had designed the banner for them on her mother's computer, and Amy and her brothers planned to hold it up when they greeted their grandparents at the airport. They were going to bring flowers, too, and Amy planned to make the supreme sacrifice of wearing the freshly cleaned and pressed pink dress.

"You don't have to worry about the house, either, Mrs. Chan," said Brittany, leaning forward from the backseat of the car as far as her seat belt would let her. "We promise to have everything cleaned up and put away long before they arrive."

"That's right," Cricket said. "The haunted house has to be open for judging between seven and nine, but we'll close it right after that and start taking things down. Mark's brother promised to load all the stuff into his pickup truck and take it back to their house tonight."

"By Saturday morning," said Meg, "it'll probably all seem like a dream!"

"A good dream, not a nightmare, I hope!" said Mrs. Chan. "Seriously, I *am* glad you girls are doing this. So is Mrs. Sanchez. She told me Mark's really happy to be working with you. He'd been so disappointed about not being able to make a haunted house this year. And it's probably helped keep me sane, too," she added, turning the car into the Chans' driveway. "At least I didn't spend all week hanging wallpaper and fussing around with dried flowers!"

That was something to be thankful for! Amy thought as she and the other girls scrambled out of the car and headed across the front lawn, where they'd soon be setting up tombstones and stringing wires for Mark's flying ghosts. She was still concerned, though, about her mother. What she really needed before Amy's grandparents arrived was a nice relaxing evening with nothing at all to worry about. But she was hardly likely to get that around here!

The phone was ringing when they came into the house and Mrs. Chan rushed to answer it, picking up the extension in the kitchen. Amy, pushing her worries about her mother to the back of her mind, headed straight for the refrigerator. "We'd better have a snack," she said, taking a container of ice cream from the freezer and passing it to Cricket, who was already getting out bowls. "We're going to need lots of energy to—" She stopped as her mother's voice, speaking into the phone, suddenly rose. She was talking to Amy's father.

"Oh, Ken, that would be wonderful!" she exclaimed. "I've been dying to see it! But how can we? This is the big night. There'll be so much going on. I don't think that Mitchell could—Of course, I want to, but . . ." She glanced quickly at Amy. "Look, Ken, let me call you back," she said.

"Mom, what is it?" Amy asked. She could tell from the look on her mother's face that it was something exciting, but Mrs. Chan tried to play it down.

"Oh, it's nothing really," she said. "That is . . . it's something, but I don't see how we can do it, so—"

"What? Do what?" Amy demanded.

"Oh, Amy, it's a play!" Mrs. Chan's eyes lit up as she said the words. "A musical called *Midnight Magic* that just opened in San Francisco. Everyone's been talking about it. It's gotten rave reviews and it's been sold out for weeks." She paused.

"So?" Amy prompted.

"So, your father says that one of the doctors in his office has a pair of tickets for tonight's show. He can't use them so he wants to give them to us. But I don't see how we can go," she said. "Your father thinks Mitchell could stay home to supervise, but I think you girls need a grown-up around."

"Then call my mother," suggested Cricket, putting down the ice cream. "I'll bet she'd come over. My dad could stay home to hand out treats at our house."

"You really shouldn't miss the chance to see that show, Mrs. Chan," said Brittany. "My parents went last week and they said it was wonderful."

"And it's just what you need," added Meg. "You've worked so hard all week helping us with this stuff."

"Go on, Mom," Amy urged. She knew how much her mother loved the theater, especially musicals, which always gave her ideas for her aerobic routines. "Call Mrs. Connors. We'll be perfectly all right here."

"Well, I don't know. I probably shouldn't, but if you're sure. . ." Mrs. Chan reached for the phone. "We'd be home as soon as it's over, by eleven o'clock at the latest," she said, the excitement returning to her voice as she dialed Cricket's number. "You girls would probably do just as well without me around worrying about things, and it wouldn't affect your grandparents' visit at all. Hello, Karen," she said as Cricket's mother came on the line. "It's Helen. I have a favor to ask . . ."

Just as Cricket had predicted, her mother said yes. After that, everything seemed to happen at once. Mrs. Chan rushed off to find something to wear. Mark and his brother Steve arrived. Alex and Brendan came home and pitched in to help. "This is a lot more fun than peeling grapes," said Alex as he strung up wires for the ghosts that would fly across the front yard.

Brittany ran around taking pictures for the scrapbook as they erected tombstones and tucked the skeleton into bed with its breakfast tray. Mitchell came home just in time to help them line the hall with Meg's velvet drapes. Much to her delight, he said he'd be glad to stay home and help Mrs. Connors supervise.

By the time Cricket's mother arrived, the girls were dressed in their witch costumes, Alex and Brendan had left for the party at the Rec Center, and Mitchell, Steve, and Mark were putting the finishing touches on the sound system that would send eerie screams and screeches, groans, and cackles echoing down the block. "I plan to hide out in the kitchen," Mrs. Connors said when Amy's mother appeared, dressed for her dinner date before the theater. "I have to make favors for a wedding tomorrow. Two hundred of them! I brought my supplies," she said, holding up the shopping bag she was carrying, "so I can work on them here."

"I don't know how you do it, Karen," said Mrs. Chan, shaking her head. "Come to think of it, I don't know how any of us do it!" She slipped on her coat, the jade-green one that Amy always thought made her look so pretty. "Now don't do anything too scary for the little kids," she warned, giving Amy a quick squeeze. "And if the phone rings be sure to answer it because it could be your grandparents calling with some change of plans."

"Mom, don't worry," said Amy, pushing her mother toward the car. "Everything's going to be fine. Just go and enjoy the play!"

The first little trick-or-treaters—the youngest ones—were coming down the block as Mrs. Chan pulled out of the drive and Cricket's mother retreated to the kitchen. Mark, who was dressed as a vampire, switched on the lights and the spooky tape recording. It wasn't dark enough yet to get the full effect of the spotlight falling on the tombstones, but it was scary enough to make the children hold their parents' hands tightly as they scurried across the yard.

"Do you think any of the moms and dads are judges?" whispered Meg to Amy as they led the first group of children and parents into the house and down the velvet-lined hall.

"Could be," said Amy. She paused outside her room and let out a witchlike cackle before pushing the door open. The kids peeked in, leaped back screaming at the sight of the skeleton having breakfast in bed, and then scampered down the hall to the family room where more horrors awaited them. "We should probably be sure to put on a good show whenever any adults—with or without kids—are around," she said. "Especially," she added, shivering at the thought, "when we do the coffin trick!"

The coffin trick, set up in the family room, was the highlight of the haunted house tour. "It was a huge success when we did it last year," Mark said when he set up the big cardboard coffin he and his brother had made. "The idea is, we take turns lying down inside it, pretending to be dead. You have to lie really still. I'll rig up a green light so it shines down on you. That'll make you look sort of unreal, like a mannequin or a big, gruesome-looking doll. Then when someone comes up to the coffin and peeks in—and they always do, they just can't resist—you suddenly sit up and open your eyes. People get totally freaked out!"

Amy couldn't wait to try it. She wasn't scheduled for coffin duty until eight-thirty, but there were plenty of other things to keep her busy—like operating the pulleys that made the ghosts fly over the tombstones in the front yard, leading blindfolded kids to the bowls of peeled grapes and cold spaghetti, and keeping an eye out for people who might be judges. She noticed a couple whispering to each other as they peeked in on the breakfast-in-bed scene. Brittany saw a man writing something in a notebook, and Cricket was certain she'd seen a woman, with a screaming child in tow, check off the Chans' address on a map. "I think she had Valerie's address checked off, too," she added. "I'd sure like to know what's going on over there."

"So would I!" said Amy. Had Valerie's set designer uncle turned the entire house into Dracula's castle? Maybe Valerie and Kristin had recruited actors from the drama society to be tour guides. Or maybe they'd hired a real live vampire. If anybody would be able to find one, it would be them!

"Do you think it's really spectacular?" she asked Mark as she finally got ready to take her turn in the coffin. "I mean Valerie and Kristin's haunted house.

Do you think they'll beat us?"

Mark, who'd just climbed out of the coffin, looked surprised. "You know, I've been having so much fun that I almost forgot about the contest," he said. "Not that I don't hope we win. Everyone's worked so hard. You've done a great job of organizing, Amy, and . . ." He took out his vampire teeth. "Well, I've really liked getting to know you," he said.

Amy, who was about to climb into the coffin, stopped. Mark had his hair slicked back and parted in the middle and there were streaks of white and green makeup on his cheeks, but his eyes were just as big and brown as ever.

"Actually, I was wondering," he went on, "if maybe you'd like to go watch football practice at the high school some afternoon. My brother's on the team. Cricket and the others could come, too," he added quickly.

Amy hesitated, not trusting herself to speak. She felt like she had at the exercise studio when she thought he wanted to ask her to go to Elmer's. Only this time he *had* asked. "Uh . . . yes, sure," she replied, trying to sound casual. "I'd like that. I like football."

Mark looked relieved, as if he'd been worried about what her reply would be. "Well . . . great!" he said. He stuck his vampire teeth back in his mouth. "Now, I'd better go check on those ghosts." He hurried out of the room, his vampire cape billowing behind him. "Sometimes the pulleys get stuck."

Scarcely noticing what she was doing, Amy climbed into the coffin. She crossed her hands over her chest, feeling her heartbeat beneath her black witch's dress. She forced herself to close her eyes, but she was afraid she wasn't going to make a very good corpse. After Mark's invitation, she felt much too alive!

In the hallway outside, she could hear trick-or-treaters whispering and giggling. Soon they'd be peeking into the bedroom and then they'd come running in here. She had to pull herself together and try to look dead. Outside the house she heard a car stop and a car door slam shut. Could it be her parents? But it was too early for them to come home. Maybe it was Mark's brother returning with the pickup truck. Or Cricket's father might have driven over to see the haunted house. Or maybe it was her grandparents. Maybe they'd caught an earlier flight. Or her mother had gotten their arrival time wrong. Now that would be something! she thought, letting her mind wander. Suppose they showed up on the doorstep just as Meg was stirring the dry ice in the big black cauldron and cackling through the rising steam. Suppose they stepped into the house through the door that the girls had decorated to look like a giant spike-toothed mouth. Suppose they found their way down the velvet-lined hall and stumbled into the cobweb-draped family room to see their granddaughter lying in a coffin, a sickly green light on her face!

"Amy!" Cricket's voice roused her from her daydream. She heard the sound of footsteps—grown-up footsteps—coming into the room. The judges! Cricket must have figured out who they were and was trying to warn her. Forgetting about her grandparents, she tightened her stomach muscles. She wished she'd had a chance to rehearse. She'd have to sit up fast, in one quick move, keeping her eyes shut until the very last moment.

"Amy, I think . . ." She heard Cricket's voice again. What was wrong with her? She was going to give the whole trick away if she kept on talking. She felt someone's presence by the coffin. She could hear breathing and then a startled gasp. This was it! One, two, three! she counted to herself. And with one swift move, she sat up and opened her eyes.

Two people stared at her, astonished.

But they weren't more astonished than Amy. It couldn't be. But it was—a scene right out of her daydream. For the horrified faces staring at her were the same as those in the picture on the mantelpiece.

"Grandma and Grandpa Chan!" Amy exclaimed. And then, because she couldn't think of anything else to say, she added crazily, "Happy Halloween!"

Chapter

The clock on the mantelpiece in the Chans' living room, next to the picture of Amy's grandparents, read 11:05 when Amy finally heard her parents' car pull into the driveway. She'd been stretched out, exhausted, along with Alex, Brendan, and Mitchell, half-watching a show on TV, but she jumped up, suddenly alert, as she heard the car doors slam. She exchanged a quick look with her brothers. She could see they were thinking the same thing. What would their parents say when they heard the news?

Amy wasn't sure, but she had a feeling it might be a lot more dramatic than any of the gasps and screams she'd heard this evening. She raced to the front door, followed by Alex and Brendan. The house was clean, except for a few cobwebs here and there. Everyone had worked hard, packing things up, moving furniture back into place, stripping the velvet drapes from the hallway.

The tombstones and ghosts were gone from the front yard, and when Mrs. Chan stepped through the door, it was clear that she couldn't believe her eyes. "Amy, I'm amazed!" she exclaimed. "It's spotless."

"I told you they'd do a fine job," said Dr. Chan. "Now aren't you glad we went to the show?"

"Oh, yes! I wish you could have seen it, Amy," Mrs. Chan said, taking off her coat and hanging it up in the hall closet. "It was wonderful! And Meg was right. It was just what I needed. I'll be totally relaxed when your grandparents arrive."

Brendan clapped his hand over his mouth. Alex turned away, his shoulders shaking. And Amy choked back a giggle.

"What is it? What's so funny?" asked their father.

"Nothing," replied Amy quickly. "Only—"

"How about Mrs. Connors?" her mother interrupted, closing the closet door. "I suppose she and Cricket have gone home. I hope you didn't give her too hard a time."

"Don't worry, we didn't," said Amy. "She managed to get all her party favors made, and then she put together a lovely meal for—" She stopped herself and glanced at her brothers who were struggling to pull themselves together.

Mrs. Chan looked surprised. "A meal? But I left plenty of stuff for sandwiches. You girls shouldn't have made Cricket's mother cook. She does enough of that in her business."

"Oh, but she wanted to," said Amy. "And besides, it

wasn't for us. You see—"

"Maybe we'd better just show them," said Mitchell, coming in from the living room. He'd taken the gold earring out of his ear and was grinning mischievously. "Mom, Dad, come on. But you'll have to be quiet."

"Why?" Amy's mother exchanged a puzzled glance with Amy's father.

"What's going on, Mitchell?" Dr. Chan said.

But Mitchell was already leading the way down the hall toward the guest bedroom. "Shh," he warned, holding his finger to his lips as he quietly pushed open the door. "We put them to bed because they were so tired. You wouldn't want to wake them." Then he and Amy, Alex, and Brendan stood aside as their parents, looking thoroughly confused, peeked into the room.

Mrs. Chan gasped, just as the little trick-or-treaters had done when they saw the skeleton in Amy's bed. Dr. Chan put his arm on her shoulder and they stepped silently into the room. The two figures lying in bed between the brand new sheets, under the brand new patchwork quilt, turned and sighed contentedly in their sleep. Amy saw her mother's eyes open wide. Though she managed not to scream, Amy was sure she was tempted. Her father looked even more astonished.

"How about a nice cup of tea?" Amy suggested, grinning at Alex and Brendan as her parents beat a hasty retreat from the room. "I think there are even some leftovers from the dinner Mrs. Connors cooked for Grandma and Grandpa!"

It was some time, and several cups of tea later, before Amy's parents recovered from the shock. "I still don't understand it," said Dr. Chan in amazement. "How could it have happened? I'm sure they said they were going to arrive tomorrow."

"Grandpa thinks Grandma got things mixed up," said Amy.

"And Grandma thinks Grandpa did," said Alex.

"And I think it had something to do with the International Date Line," Brendan put in. "We just learned about it in geography. It's in the middle of the Pacific Ocean and when you cross it going east, you lose a day, or maybe it's the other way around and you gain a day. Anyway, the date changes and it's pretty confusing."

Amy's mother shook her head. "What must they have thought?" she said, for what seemed like the hundredth time. "Arriving at the airport with no one to meet them, having to take a cab all the way here. I don't understand why they didn't phone, though. If they had, Mitchell could have gone to pick them up."

"Uh . . . well . . ." Mitchell looked embarrassed. "Apparently they did try to call, but the line was busy. I guess I was talking to Cindy," he said. Cindy was Mitchell's girlfriend. "I didn't realize we were on the phone for so long."

"Oh, Mitchell," Mrs. Chan sighed. "This is *so* embarrassing."

"No it's not, Helen," Dr. Chan assured her. "It's just

one of those things that will make a good family story. We'll all be laughing about it tomorrow. They must have been pretty surprised by the haunted house."

"Oh, they were," said Amy, remembering the look on her grandmother's face when she'd sprung up from the coffin. "But they're so nice. Even though they were tired after the plane trip, and confused about the mix-up, when we explained what was going on they seemed to understand. They wanted to wait up to see you, but by the time Cricket's mother had made them something to eat, and we'd all pitched in to clean things up, they were exhausted. We thought they should just go to bed."

"And that's what I think we should all do now!" declared Mrs. Chan. "But first—" She glanced at Amy's father. "We'd better tell you about someone we met at the theater tonight, Amy."

"At the theater?"

"Ah, yes," said her father, suddenly looking serious. "I'd almost forgotten. We met your teacher, Amy. Mr. Crockett. He said something about a letter."

The letter! Amy saw Alex and Brendan exchange a glance. They knew about letters sent home from school. "Oh no! I forgot!" she exclaimed. "That is, I didn't at first. But then when we started planning the haunted house . . ." But she could see from the look on her parents' faces that there was no point in making excuses. Though by now she was so tired she could barely keep her eyes open, she ran to her room and dug the backpack out of her closet. She found the envelope inside, only slightly stained with chocolate.

"Thank you," said her father when she handed it to him. He didn't open it, though. "Now let's all get some sleep. We can talk about this in the morning."

Amy's eyes closed almost the moment she hit the pillow. But she didn't sleep very soundly. All night long she had the most incredible dreams. She was flying over her house on a broomstick with her grandparents hanging on behind. Down below, a football team was scrimmaging on the front lawn and Mark was on the sidelines cheering, with Valerie and Kristin beside him. She tried to land the broom, but she couldn't. And then her grandparents disappeared and Mr. Crockett was on the broomstick behind her, waving the haunted house flyer at her parents, who were doing a dance on the roof. Her father looked up and began shouting, "No more soccer! No more club! No more anything, Amy! Amy! Amy!"

She felt like she was tumbling from her broomstick, falling down, down, down. She gripped the sides of her bed, but the motion didn't stop. Suddenly her eyes opened and she realized that someone was shaking her. "Amy! Amy!" It was Cricket's voice. "Wake up, Amy! It's almost lunchtime."

She saw Cricket's freckled face looking down at her. Behind her stood Brittany and Meg. "Oh, I was having the craziest dream!" she exclaimed, sitting up and running a hand through her tangled hair. "I was flying on a broomstick and my grandparents were there, and Mr. Crockett, and even Valerie and—But what's the matter?" All at once she noticed the expression on her friends' faces. You look so—Oh no!" she said. "Is it the contest? Did we . . . I mean, didn't we . . ." She let her voice trail off, not wanting to say the words.

Cricket nodded. "That's right. We didn't win. Meg just found out from a friend of her grandmother's who's on the Chamber of Commerce board. When we phoned, your mother said she wanted to let you sleep because you'd been up so late last night, but we just had to come over. It didn't seem fair for you to not know about it when we did."

Amy sank back on her pillows. In a way, she wasn't surprised. She hadn't had much time to think about winning lately, with so many other things going on. But now . . . "I guess we'll never hear the end of it," she groaned. "Valerie and Kristin will rub it in every chance they get!"

"Oh, but it wasn't them," said Brittany. "They didn't win."

"They didn't?" Amy said. "Then who . . ."

"Someone on Sycamore Avenue," Meg replied. "I guess we were all so focused on Valerie and Kristin that we never even thought about anyone else winning the prize. Two hundred dollars," she said wistfully. "I certainly hope they have something good to spend it on."

"Oh, Meg." Amy saw the disappointed look on Meg's face and remembered about Jenny. "I'm so sorry. It's all my fault. I should have thought of a better project, one that didn't depend on winning."

"But it wasn't just you," Meg said quickly. "We all wanted to do it. I wish we had won so I'd have the money to bring Jenny up for Christmas. But if you'd thought up a different project, we would never have had so much fun."

"And I might never have taken such great pictures," said Brittany. "I'm going to get the film developed right away so we can put them in the scrapbook. It's going to look terrific! And besides," she added, a mysterious look on her face, "Meg is going to get her money. And you, too, Amy. It's my turn to think up a project, and I have one in mind that could more than make up for what we didn't earn this time."

"You do? Brittany, what is it?" said Cricket. "Can we do it before Thanksgiving? That would give Meg plenty of time to get a plane ticket. Come on. Don't be mean. Tell us what it is."

But Brittany wouldn't. "Not yet," she said. "I'm not absolutely sure about it. You'll just have to be patient and wait for the next meeting."

The meeting! An alarm seemed to go off in Amy's head at the sound of that word. She remembered her dream—the part where her father was standing on the roof, looking up at her and yelling, "No more soccer! No more club!" She thought of the chocolate-stained envelope she'd handed him last night. Her parents must have read the letter inside it by now. They must have decided what they were going to do with her. But she couldn't give up the club! She couldn't let them make her do that. Leaping out of bed, she grabbed her bathrobe from the closet. "Are my mom and dad both here?" she asked.

"Yes. Everyone's in the kitchen," Cricket replied, not seeming to notice the expression on Amy's face. "Your grandmother's making some kind of wonderful dumplings and your mother invited all of us to stay for lunch. They seem to be getting along just fine," she added. "I heard your grandmother say that this is a beautiful house and that your mother has excellent taste. And guess what? Brittany was talking to your grandfather and she found out that his factory supplies fabric to her mother's company. She's even been to Hong Kong! Brittany, I mean."

"Oh, but it was just for a short time," said Brittany quickly, looking faintly embarrassed, as she always did whenever any part of the glamorous life she had led was revealed. "My mother went there on a business trip. My nanny was on vacation, so I had to go along."

At any other time, Amy would have been interested in hearing about Brittany's travels—and about how she'd had a nanny!—but right now, she didn't care. "Come on," she said, motioning for the girls to follow as she slipped on her bathrobe and headed down the hall. "You've got to back me up. I'll get a tutor, I'll study every day, I'll even give up soccer. But I'm not—*I'm absolutely not*—going to give up the Always Friends Club!"

"Give up the club? What are you talking about, Amy?" said Cricket as they rushed into the kitchen. "Who would want you to do that?"

"No one would," said Dr. Chan, answering Cricket's question. He was leaning back in his chair at the kitchen table, alongside Amy's grandfather, watching Grandma Chan roll out little rounds of dough and fill them with chopped shrimp and vegetables. Through the window, Amy could see her brothers tossing a football around in the backyard.

"Ah, Amy," said Grandma Chan, her eyes crinkling up in a smile. "You look very different this morning."

"Much healthier," said Grandpa Chan, chuckling. "Not so good for a girl to sleep in a coffin."

In spite of herself, Amy smiled. She knew she was going to enjoy her grandparents' visit. She'd show them all around Redwood Grove. Maybe she'd even take them to Elmer's. But right now, she had to find out about that letter. "What did it say?" she demanded, looking at her father and then at her mother. "What did Mr. Crockett tell you?"

"Ah, so that's what you're worried about," said Mrs. Chan. She opened the sliding glass door for Midnight, who was meowing outside, after having wisely disappeared while the house was being haunted. "The letter is not what you think it is, Amy."

"It's not?" said Amy. Midnight dashed inside and began to rub happily against her pajama-clad leg. "You mean I didn't fail those tests?"

"Quite the contrary," said her father. "In fact, you did so well on the spatial intelligence section that Mr. Crockett is recommending you for a special enrichment program. That's what the letter was about. You should have given it to us right away, Amy. But I suppose with all that's been going on around here you can be forgiven for forgetting."

Amy was stunned. An enrichment program? Spatial intelligence? She didn't even know what that was!

"Gosh, Amy," said Cricket, looking impressed. "Does that mean you're some kind of genius?"

"It means she has a strong ability to visualize things," Dr. Chan explained. "It's the kind of intelligence architects and engineers need. Airplane pilots, too."

Now Amy was doubly stunned. An airplane pilot? Maybe that's why she'd been dreaming about flying. She thought of all those designs she'd made for the haunted house, of how she'd built castles out of blocks in nursery school, and how she loved using Mitchell's graph paper. Was that what it all meant? It was hard to imagine. She'd always thought of herself as someone with a good, strong body who could play sports for hours, but she'd never dreamed there was anything special about her brain! "Gee," she said, sinking down on one of the chairs by the table where her grandmother was making dumplings.

"You'd better not let it go to your head," teased Meg. "We don't want you to start thinking you're too good for the club."

Her words brought Amy back to the present. "Then I won't have to give it up, will I?" she said, looking at her parents. "The Always Friends Club, I mean."

"Of course not," said Mrs. Chan. "I don't know where you could have gotten such an idea. I think you girls are going to be doing things together for a long, long time. Why, the club is the best thing that—" She was interrupted by the ringing of the phone.

Dr. Chan, who was closest to the receiver, picked it up. "Amy, it's for you," he said. "Someone named Mark."

Cricket and Meg exchanged a glance. Brittany looked worried. "Cricket . . ." she warned.

But Amy wasn't going to give any of them a chance to tease her. "I'll take it in the other room," she said quickly, hurrying out of the kitchen to pick up the extension in the family room. Mark's voice came over the line. Amy flopped down on the sofa and put her feet up on the coffee table, just as Mitchell did when he was talking to Cindy.

"I'm sorry we lost," Mark said after she'd told him about the house on Sycamore Avenue winning the contest. "But I'm not sorry we did it. It was lots of fun. And don't forget about football practice," he reminded her. "We could go Monday after school if you'd like. Ask the others, too."

"Sure," said Amy, wiggling her toes. "But they may not want to come." And who knows? she thought. They may not even get asked! After all, even friends who are always friends don't have to do everything together!